Dust motes danced in a feeble ray of light filtering down onto the stage.

Mrs. Outhwaite was saying, "We've made the hayloft into a musicians' gallery. Sometimes we have a small musical group there."

She stopped and they all three stood and gazed at the figure on the stage. Michaela, too rapt to have heard them come in, was dancing as if bewitched by her own imagination. Julia glanced at Laura. They both remembered the courtyard at the pension and Michaela's solitary dancing. Her movements now were more certain, more vigorous, as if she was emboldened by the greater space, the smooth boards under her feet.

Mrs. Outhwaite, who had stood watching, speechless, suddenly called out, "Michaela!" Her voice rang out in the vaulted quiet and the girl on the stage stopped instantly and stood motionless, as if struck.

Julia watched Michaela's swift change from a vibrant figure moving with charged energy to a docile, half-frightened girl. She stepped slowly off the stage and walked down the length of the barn towards them. As she stood quietly in front of them, with her head bowed, Laura said gently, "You do so want to dance, don't you, Michaela?"

To

TW

Twenty years ago The Naiad Press published its first book, my novel *The Latecomer*. Since then books from Naiad have done much to transform the world for lesbian readers. Some of them have been landmarks in the history of the publishing of lesbian literature.

It seems appropriate to me that this anniversary should be marked by the publication of my latest novel *Michaela*.

SARAH ALDRIDGE

Michaela

BY
SARAH
ALDRIDGE

The Naiad Press, Inc.
1994

Printed in the United States of America on acid-free paper
First Edition

Cover design by Pat Tong and Bonnie Liss
    (Phoenix Graphics)
Typeset by Sandi Stancil

Library of Congress Cataloging-in-Publication Data

Aldridge, Sarah.
    Michaela / by Sarah Aldridge.
        p.   cm.
    ISBN 1-56280-055-8
    1. Lesbians—Fiction.   I. Title.
PS3551.L345M48   1994
813'.54—dc20   93-41788
                                                                CIP

I

The girl was climbing the cobbled street, which was flanked on either side by high stone walls. They were old walls, crumbled in places and sprouting green shoots and seedlings, overtopped by tall trees in the gardens behind them, which threw a dense shade dappled here and there by beams of sunlight. Except for the girl, the street was empty. In the middle of the afternoon there was little movement in this quiet neighborhood; its once great mansions were now chiefly pensions for traveling foreigners.

"Remnant of another day, isn't it?" said Laura,

seated in the window of the big house at the top of the street.

"Yes," said Julia, looking over her head. "That's why we are here. The ad specified that this was an old-world town and that the inn was once the home of one of Napoleon III's physicians. We told the travel agency that we wanted to see the chateaux but we also wanted to stay somewhere off the beaten track, where we could spend two or three weeks, no great distance from Paris. Yes, I can believe that Empress Eugenie might have visited here, accompanied by her ladies in white crinolines and satin pelisses and little hats covered in rosebuds — like a flock of brilliant birds coming to rest on the terrace down there."

Laura smiled up at her. "Yes, of course. The Winterhalter portrait. Madame Guerin even has a reproduction hanging in the lounge downstairs — the swelling bosoms, the bejeweled hands holding fans. Madame says the buses will come on the weekends, but hopes we shall not be disturbed." Laura's gaze was still fixed on the scene below them.

"What are you looking at?" Julia demanded.

"The girl." Laura pointed out of the window. "She does this every afternoon. How old would you say she is? Fourteen?"

Julia studied the girl climbing the steep street. She was sturdy, dressed in a white blouse and dark blue jumper, white socks and black shoes. A school uniform, such as all French schoolgirls wore. She was carrying a canvas sack with straps for handles, obviously heavy. She was stopping now, setting the sack down on the cobbles and resting by leaning her back against the wall, looking down the hill, as if watching something out of sight of the two women in the window. Presently she picked up the sack and started up the hill again. She moved slowly but there was a purposefulness to her plodding, nothing lax or impatient in the stance of her body.

Laura said impulsively, "A kid like that shouldn't be so patient!"

Julia, who had turned away, came back and looked over Laura's head again. "You mean, she should be dragging that sack along, the way a sulky child would. Probably she'd get a hiding when she got home if she did."

"But she doesn't look as if she's fearful. She acts like a grown person — somebody — somebody —"

"Who's suffered the slings and arrows of misfortune. Well, maybe."

The girl had almost reached the top of the street and was close enough for them to see her face distinctly. It was a long face with full lips and a prominent nose, framed by dark hair that was held back in a clasp. Her skin was a smooth, unblemished olive. Another step or two would bring her under the wall of the Auberge Celestin, in whose window they sat, and out of their sight.

"She looks like a gypsy," said Julia.

"Can she belong here? I've not seen her in the house."

"Perhaps she works here, in the kitchen. The French are good about that. They make all the children go to school, whether they're French or not. But on the other hand — you know, there is a door in the wall of that shabby place next door, just where it joins Mme. Guerin's. Madame complains about that house. It's so badly kept that it lets down

3

the tone of the neighborhood, she thinks. And that would affect the tourist trade."

"I'll ask her at dinner tonight."

"Ask her what?"

"About the girl."

Julia looked at her, alerted by her preoccupation. Laura was fair-haired and pale, a pallor which Julia knew had been accentuated by the events of the past year — the events that had been the reason for this holiday — this brief little interlude away from the sources of responsibility, so that she might recover some of the cheerful vigor that was normally hers. It was always with a pang that Julia noticed this evidence of sorrow and frustration.

They were the only guests at the dinner table that evening. Madame Guerin's house, being not so far from Paris, attracted a good many overnight guests and people who came for a weekend in the country. But in the middle of the week there were often days without visitors. Mme. Guerin sat now at the head of the table, a good-looking, middle-aged widow, plump and brisk. She had bought the house to run as a business, she said, and claimed no descent from Louis Napoleon's physician, though she cultivated the legend of visits by the Empress Eugenie as a romantic draw for tourists.

She was puzzled by Laura's question. What girl? Oh, the child next door. There was an expression of mixed annoyance and resignation on her face. Such unhandy sort of people. Of course, one must sympathize with their misfortunes. There were so many of them, these foreigners coming as refugees from everywhere, one sometimes was overwhelmed.

"I try to help Madame Souza," Mme. Guerin said

4

with a pursed mouth. "But it is difficult. She has not been here very long."

"Do you mean that they also take travelers?" asked Laura.

Madame Guerin shrugged. "Yes, of course — when they can get them. Sometimes, when I have a full house and am faced with unexpected arrivals — some people are very improvident in making arrangements for a holiday and have nowhere to spend the night — I send them to Madame Souza. Her rooms arc clean and you will not suffer any inconvenience. But of course there is nothing like this" — she made an all-encompassing gesture over the dinner spread before them. "For one thing, she has no grasp of what is required if you are to give people this kind of service." Mme. Guerin had lapsed into French, finding English inadequate for expressing the depth of her contempt. Julia had pointed out to Laura that, though her English was entirely adequate for dealing with her guests, she relaxed in the evenings with those who spoke French — like taking off her shoes at the end of the day.

"What is her misfortune?" Laura persisted.

Mme. Guerin shrugged again. "The same as with all of them — no country of their own, no means of livelihood, no training for employment. There are so many like them these days. I am not in Madame Souza's confidence. I do not know the details of her personal history. She comes from Portugal but it is apparent to me that she is not Portuguese. During the Occupation, in the war, we had people like that. They were taken away by the authorities. They disappeared, you understand. At the time we — ordinary people like myself — we had no means of knowing what became of such people. That came later, after the war and the news of the concentration camps." The embarrassment of seeming to apologize for the national disgrace added a tone of resentment to her voice.

Laura asked, "Then they are Jewish?"

Julia added, "Or gypsies?"

"I have no information. It is an impression I have. They are not French, though they speak fluently, but not correctly. The girl perhaps better, since she goes to school here. I would not say that Madame Souza is Jewish or a gypsy."

The curious limitation to what she said struck both of them. On the way up to bed later Julia said, "The girl could be a gypsy."

"She is very vivid," said Laura.

"She has made an impression on you, hasn't she?"

The weekend brought an influx of visitors, busloads of people traveling in conducted tours to see the chateaux. Laura and Julia found themselves surrounded by throngs.

"Perhaps we should leave now," Julia grumbled.

"They'll be gone by Monday," said Laura, soothingly. "And I like it here. The weather is glorious."

At dinner, which they ate at a small table squeezed into a corner next to the door to the kitchen, they watched the crowd in the dining room, more diverted than they had expected to be. They were so entertained, in fact, that it came as a surprise when their attention was caught by a soft voice saying, "Mesdames, some more peas, more truite aux herbes?"

The girl was standing at Laura's elbow, so that she had to turn to see her. But Julia was staring at her across the table. She seemed not to notice. Conquering her surprise, Laura said, "You are new here. I have not seen you before."

The girl's eyelashes fluttered briefly. She had long black eyelashes that swept down over her dark eyes. She said, "I am here to help Madame Guerin. She has so many people. She did not expect so many."

Her voice was pitched low and after a first glance at Laura she dropped her eyes and kept them fixed on the dishes she was offering. In a moment she was gone, passing on to another table and they did not see her again.

In their room, where they went soon after to escape the crowded lounge, Julia said, "Yoo, she could be a gypsy."

"You mean because of her looks. But she doesn't act like one — certainly not like those we saw in Paris, begging for money. She seems very demure — meek, in fact. She was very careful handling the dishes, as if she wasn't used to waiting on table."

"Probably the first time she has waited on table — afraid of dropping something. If she did, Madame probably would be harsh — even if she hired her because she could pay her less than anybody else she could get in an emergency."

"Oh, Julia!" Laura remonstrated. "After all, Madame said she tries to help the girl's mother. This is one of those occasions when she needs help and goes next door for it."

Julia's amusement showed at the corners of her mouth. How handsome she is, thought Laura, her attention distracted by a sudden leap of fondness for Julia. People find her formidable — that bold air of self-confidence, but I know she is lovable.

"Well, there is always the French sense of self-interest. It invariably tempers their compassion."

Laura, following her own train of thought, said, "But there is a certain feeling of — wildness about her. Underneath, as if something runs deeper than the submissiveness."

"The girl, you mean? Wildness? I thought she was a little clumsy. I don't mean because she is not a trained servant. I mean, a sort of innate clumsiness, as if she is not naturally clever with her hands." Julia paused and then asked, "Then you don't want to leave — flee from this crowd?"

"No," said Laura. "I want to know more about this girl."

Julia sighed and looked at Laura. Laura, so tolerant and undemanding most of the time — too undemanding, as she had often complained in the past. But then she could put her foot down and that was that.

Monday came and the Auberge Celestin was once more almost empty, and their meals were served by the middle-aged maid. As usual Madame came to sit at their table and chat.

Laura said, "You had a very busy weekend. Do you expect more visitors?"

Madame sighed with an air of complaint that was underlain with satisfaction. "This Wednesday a party of American professors will come. Poor Mathilde will be run off her legs. I shall have to have the little one from next door to come and help again."

"She is very willing," said Laura.

Madame grimaced. "Yes, certainly. She is amiable. If she were only competent."

"You don't find her so?" Laura is leading her on, thought Julia.

"Necessity often makes us eager when we might not otherwise be. She will always come when I need her. Her mother needs whatever money she can earn."

"Are you saying that she is not a good servant?"

Again Madame grimaced. "I do not say that, no. She is untrained." Her expression changed from disapproving to thoughtful. "It seems sometimes that she is not capable of learning the little niceties. She is clumsy — something she cannot overcome even with her eagerness. If she was negligent — willfully careless — that I could understand. But she tries hard, without success."

"Does she break things?"

"Not that bad. Occasionally, she does, but that is acceptable. But it is as if she has never been taught now to do the essential things — what pot to use, how to prepare the vegetables, the proper way to set the tables."

"Probably she has not been taught."

"But, Madame, what kind of a mother is it that does not teach her daughter the essentials of life? And a sensible girl, a girl who has been in many places, must have seen how things are done. You, for instance, Madame, would know that you do not dump all the silverware in a heap by the plate. You would know where to store the milk, how to preserve the cheese. She tries, certainly, to do what needs to be done and she obeys when you instruct her but you can see that she does not always understand and therefore she makes the same mistake another time."

"Then she must not be used to living as we do — she has not learned our formalities. Is she, then, really a gypsy?

Madame Guerin seemed checked by the question. "I do not know. I do not speculate. Her mother seems a different sort altogether. She is a woman who is accustomed to our formalities, as you call them. In fact, I would say that she has been someone's housekeeper, someone's maid. But a superior sort. It is very strange."

"What is the girl's name?" Julia asked.

"Michaela — as if she were Portuguese. But her mother is the very type of an Englishwoman. And she does not neglect the daughter. She is strict with her."

Laura said, "We see her in the afternoons, climbing up the hill with a sack of things. She must go to the village."

"She goes to school and when she returns she brings whatever her mother needs from the village. Her mother never goes down to the village. She dislikes dealing with the shopkeepers. Michaela works very hard, especially when they have some guests. Her mother has no other servant."

"And she comes to you when you need extra help," Julia said.

Mme. Guerin, as if sensing an unstated criticism, answered briskly, "The money is very necessary to them. I could hire a village girl. There are plenty of them eager to come to the Auberge Celestin."

"Oh, I am sure of that!" said Laura, quick to assuage Mme. Guerin's wounded pride. "But if she is so unsatisfactory —"

Mme. Guerin said hastily, "Oh, she is very honest. She is not a thief. She never cheats when she deals with money. She is not like a gypsy at all when it comes to that."

"But," said Laura, "how can her mother spare her to you when she herself has a house full of guests?"

Mme. Guerin was nonplussed for a moment and then seemed to understand the question. "Ah! Mme. Souza does not offer a complete table to her guests. She provides breakfast and can prepare picnic lunches for those who wish to take food with them when they go out sightseeing for the day. She is not foolish enough to suppose that she could offer adequate dinners. Her guests come to me for their main meals." Mme. Guerin surveyed the dining room with a lofty glance of self-confidence.

In their own room later Julia remarked, "She undoubtedly gets Michaela cheaper, obviously."

"And perhaps a good feeling that she is doing the right thing," Laura replied. "After all, France is overrun with refugees of one sort and another."

As Mme. Guerin predicted, on Wednesday a tour bus arrived filled with American academics. Julia, watching from the window of their room said, "We could be among them, couldn't we?"

"You, perhaps," said Laura.

"Well, I recognize the type of my colleagues. None of them are from New York, I understand. I don't suppose I'll know any of them."

At dinner that evening they sat in their corner

and watched the crowded room. Michaela came presently to their table with a tray of appetizers. She responded shyly to their greetings, as if disconcerted at being recognized — as if, thought Laura, she would rather distance herself psychologically from the people she waited on.

Laura said, "What do you recommend?"

The girl glanced briefly at her. "I cannot say, madame." Her manner was not a rebuff but it was not gracious.

When she had gone on to the next table, Laura said, "She's simply not been trained. Mme. Guerin says she's gauche. She just doesn't know how to respond."

"A gypsy, Madame said. Gypsies are not known for their social graces. They live in caravans — that's what you English call them, isn't it? Not in houses."

"But wouldn't that be a little strange in this day and time?"

"Not really. Do you remember the girl in the train station in Rome, who stood behind a pillar trying to give us the evil eye because we did not give her as much money as she wanted? And Paris is full of them."

"Like ants running in all directions when you disturb their anthill. The upheavals of these times, I suppose."

The busload of American professors paused only a day or two. When they left, Mme. Guerin's house relapsed into tranquility.

"Let's go down into the village," said Laura. "We'll have the shops to ourselves again."

Coming back from their visit to the hairdresser,

the pharmacy, they reached the steep, cobble-stoned street that led up the hill to the Auberge Celestin.

Halfway up Julia exclaimed, "Well, look up there!"

Laura raised her head to look up the hill. "My, it's Michaela! Of course. She is late. Shall we call to her?"

"No." Julia's response was quick. "She would think she had to chat with us and somehow I don't think Mme. Guerin would like that."

"I don't think she would chat with anyone, more's the pity."

"Why do you think that?"

"She's too solitary."

"What do you mean by that? We have seen her under very restricted circumstances. We've no idea what she is like when she's on her own."

"True. But I just don't think so. We'll never catch up to her unless we call to her. I'm sure I can't climb this hill as fast as she does. See how quick she is today. I'm sure she has seen us and wants to get out of the way."

"Well, let's stop for a moment," Julia said, looking anxiously at Laura. "You know you're not supposed to overdo."

They rested for a while. As they watched, the girl set her sack down and leaned against the wall. She had stopped close to the top of her climb. The wooden door in the wall opened and a woman came out, pausing as if in search of something. She was of middle height, neither fat nor thin, with nondescript blondish hair, perhaps mixed with grey, wearing a cotton dress and an apron. When she saw

Michaela — who, at sight of her had picked up her sack — she called out. They could hear her shrill voice and that she spoke in English but not what she said.

"She's scolding her," said Laura.

"I told you she must be late."

They watched as the girl reached the door in the wall and followed the woman inside. As they resumed their climb, Laura said, "Do you suppose that's her mother?"

"I suppose so. But she's ginger-haired and scrawny. Perhaps Michaela is a changeling. She's so dark and glowing and the woman is so pale and washed-out."

"And harried." There was reproof in Laura's voice.

"With reason," Julia agreed, "if what Mme. Guerin says is true — scratching a living at something she does not do well."

They reached the gravel drive of the Auberge Celestin without further talk. In their room, taking off the straw hat she wore against the sun, Laura said, "Do you suppose we could invite Michaela to come and visit us?"

Julia, surprised, asked, "Why?"

"Because I want to know more about her."

Julia's dark eyebrows drew down. "Do you think that's a good idea?"

"Why not?" Laura's blue eyes fixed on Julia's.

Julia hesitated, as usual unsettled by Laura's determination. "Well, we'll be here only a short time longer. If we befriend Michaela — that's what you have in mind, isn't it? — she will be left behind, perhaps with hopes aroused that cannot be satisfied."

Laura smiled. "I've led you into quite a lot of

14

situations, haven't I, darling? No, I don't intend to stir up that sort of trouble. But if I don't learn more about this girl, I'll remember her with regret the rest of my life."

"What?" There was alarm in Julia's voice. "Oh, Laura, why do you get so caught up by things? Besides, you know it is dangerous — dealing with a kid that age. At that age they're full of half-formed ideas — full of feelings, without clear thoughts. You're sorry for her because you think her mother overworks her. But with a girl like that, reality is far away. Don't you remember yourself at that age?"

"Yes, but I think Michaela has had a much bigger dose of reality than you or I had at that age."

"Hm," said Julia picking up her handbag and putting it on the top shelf of the clothes press that filled the corner of the room. "What pretext would you use to invite her here?"

"I don't know. I need your help there."

"It must be something that does not arouse her mother's attention — and cupidity — two well-to-do middle-aged women, you know. Something that would allow Michaela to earn a little extra money. That would have an appeal, I'm sure. Is there something we can ask Mme. Guerin if Michaela could do for us?"

"Clever of you, Julia — as is so often the case. Yes, the lure of money. Though of course you can hardly blame the woman. I think they must have been living from hand to mouth for some time. Do you suppose Mme. Guerin has some further bits of information she can give us?"

But when they next saw Mme. Guerin, the landlady obviously had something on her mind. As they chatted she kept glancing at Laura, her bright quick eyes alight with curiosity. Laura seemed not to notice. But then, thought Julia, Laura was well-schooled in maintaining an air of bland indifference.

Finally, Mme. Guerin could refrain no longer. "Mme. Houghton," she said to Laura, "did you recognize any of those people who were here — the group, you know — all Americans."

Laura returned her stare. "Why, no. Perhaps Julia —"

She glanced at Julia but Julia shook her head. "I know some of them by reputation. They've written books in their specialties. But I don't know them personally."

Mme. Guerin gave a delighted little laugh. "Ah, but they knew you, madame! Or at least your husband. He was very well-known everywhere, of course. Even I had heard of him. Silly of me not to connect you with him by your name. All those many times on the television — he was there, telling us all about it. A very remarkable man — a most courageous man. And so young — only just in his forties. I must offer you my condolences. It was a great shock to everyone that he died. Please accept my sympathy."

Laura's face turned to stone. Julia said hastily, summoning up all her resources in the French language to be diplomatic, "You understand, madame, that my friend is still in the first stage of her grief. It is difficult for her to speak of his death. Yes, he was very well known, and among Americans

16

especially. We have come on this little holiday to help her recover — away from places where she might be recognized."

Mme. Guerin made little soothing sounds, patting Laura's arm, trying to disguise the gratification that she felt that her inn had been chosen for the sojourn of the widow of yet another renowned person; she kept a roster of distinguished guests which she displayed in the lounge. But she was not quite finished. "And you, too, madame. You have your fame. You are a writer, aren't you? I am told you are widely published."

Laura managed to nod.

"Whew!" said Julia, when she left them.

* * * * *

In the dark of the night, quiet like its neighbors standing among the trees of their gardens, Mme. Guerin's house was murmurous with unidentifiable sounds, the muted creaks and groans that old houses were wont to give off. Laura, lying in the crook of Julia's arm, said sleepily, "Is it really necessary for us to leave this village, this house, this hill?"

Julia, a little startled, replied, "I hadn't thought you liked it that much — especially now that Madame knows you are Dick's widow. It's not our own place, after all — what we've been waiting for for fifteen years."

"As you always remind me. So much of our lives gone."

"And yet we're still not going back to New York

to stay, to be on our own. We are going to Sutford, you say, in Virginia, to visit the Houghtons. Why must we? It isn't as if they are your own parents. They are Dick's and I doubt that they need you as much as you think they do. There they are, in the same house they've always lived in, in the same place where they've lived forever."

"I know, I know. You won't accept it. But it's his mother. It is because of her. I admit it is sheer selfishness. It's on my own behalf that I'm doing it. I don't want to feel guilty. After all, I did love him once. I thought I loved him with all my heart and soul. Something like that can't just fade away and leave no trace. If I walk away now, before Dick is cold in his grave, as they say, as if I am really only too glad he is gone — I could never justify myself to his mother."

"Do you need to?"

"Yes. All these years she has clung to me, because she could not cling to him. I would always feel her silent reproach, no matter how many miles there were between us."

Julia stirred with indignation. "It's emotional blackmail, that's what it is."

"She's not aware of that."

"So we go on indefinitely —"

"No, not indefinitely. Just for a little while longer. They did not come to London while he was dying. I kept them away. I did not want them to know what he was dying of. You know all about that. And afterwards I said I could not come at once to see them. I had to have a rest. But now I must go and stay a little while with them, till they get used to the new situation. And you must come with me. I can't do any more without you."

Julia was silent for a while. Then she asked, "Dick never said he wanted a divorce, did he?"

"No. That was the last thing he wanted. He had it much better the other way."

"And why didn't you tell him that you wanted a divorce?"

"You know why. I did not want the notoriety. His parents would have been horrified. And he begged me not to. Julia, you know all this. Why do you make me repeat it?"

"To turn the knife in my own wound, I suppose. And to say what you are not saying: That he knew what we meant to each other and that he would have spread the news far and wide. Subtly, of course, by innuendo. So you preserved your image of the devoted and loving wife — never betrayed, never betraying — when everybody knew he chased every attractive woman who crossed his path."

"You needn't sound so bitter. I could not do anything else. I was committed. And now we're free and we haven't any skeleton rattling in our cupboards."

The next morning was fine, sunlit, as the days had been during all their stay. Their sitting room, facing east was bright and fresh with the morning breeze. Laura, coming into it, said, "Mme. Guerin says it is arranged. Michaela will come this afternoon, when she gets home from school, to serve our tea in here and tidy up afterwards. We will pay

Mme. Guerin a few extra francs, half of which will go to Michaela. It will be much more pleasant than going down to the lounge, don't you think?"

Julia put down the Paris newspaper she was reading. "Of course. There was no trouble making the arrangement?"

"No. As you suggested, the offer of money did the trick."

Julia pointed to a letter lying on the table. "There is mail for you — forwarded from London."

Laura felt a twinge of dismay as she picked up the envelope. It bore an American stamp. She opened it and drew out the two sheets of fine linen letter paper and read what her mother-in-law had written. When she had finished she stood still, holding them in her hand. She felt Julia's eyes on her.

"They want me back at once, they say. Dick's been dead a month. They need me to help them settle their lives again. They cannot wait any longer. She means herself, of course. I think my father-in-law can manage very well, but he is concerned about her."

"So what are you going to do?"

"I shall write and say that I'll be back soon — with you." Laura spoke softly. "We've been out of sight of the newsmongers long enough to avoid publicity now, I suppose."

After several minutes' thought, Laura said, "In the meantime, there's Michaela."

"You've made that arrangement."

"Yes, we'll stay another few days."

Julia studied her face but did not reply. Laura's thoughts were far away. Since Dick's death Julia had trod warily, knowing that Laura in her hypersensitive state was vulnerable to the least pressure, the least failure of compassion. Michaela, now. What was it about Michaela that had aroused such a strong wish to rescue the girl? Rescue her from circumstances over which she had no control — as Laura herself had had no control as Dick's wife.

Julia said, "I hope the girl can respond to what you offer."

"We shall see," said Laura, equably, the little storm of distress past.

The afternoon was hot and fair, the morning freshness blooming into warmth under the ardor of the sun. In their sitting room, protected by the thick stone walls of the house, it was cooler, and a light air stirred the white curtains in the greenish light filtering through the tree leaves.

"I think I hear Michaela now," said Laura.

In the corridor outside their room there was the sound of china clinking and then a knock on the door. At Laura's "Entrez," it opened and Michaela was revealed, maneuvering the tea trolley through the doorway. She nodded to the two women and stood awkwardly waiting.

Laura smiled and said, "Put it here, Michaela," pointing to the space in front of the window. "You have the hot water and the milk?"

"Yes, madame." Michaela's voice was uncharacteristically deep, surprising in such a young girl, and her French, thought Julia, was peculiar to herself, though in general it undoubtedly sounded like that of the village children.

Laura said, seeing her stand irresolute, "You needn't wait, Michaela. Come back in an hour or so."

21

Michaela, obviously relieved, nodded again in the same offhand manner and walked out of the door, closing it behind her. Laura, catching Julia's expression, laughed. "You see what Mme. Guerin means."

"She certainly has no gift for gracious service."

"She intrigues me no end. Where does she come from? Where did she grow up? It's as if her mother had never taught her anything."

"Perhaps she hasn't."

"But why? Are they really mother and daughter? There is no physical resemblance between them."

"There's no question about that, according to Mme. Guerin. Their papers are in order. I am sure Mme. Guerin would not have dealings with anyone whose identification documents were not in order."

"I've asked Mme. Guerin some more questions about her. She is reluctant to talk about them. The mother is undoubtedly English — she looked so, from what I could see of her — but not coming to France from England. Married to a foreigner? Not Algerian, says Madame. That she is certain of, though physically that is what Michaela could be. A gypsy? But, says Madame, she is honest and hardworking and not dirty — How these stereotypes cling!"

An hour later, with surprising promptness, there was a tap on the door, which opened before Laura could say Enter, and Michaela walked into the room. Without speaking to them, she began at once to gather up the cups and saucers and pile the tea things onto the tray. She was about to move the trolley when Laura stopped her.

"Michaela, how long have you lived here?"

Michaela looked surprised. "Here —?"

"In France."

A sudden shyness seemed to overwhelm Michaela. She mumbled, "I don't remember."

"Since you were a little girl, then?"

Distress obvious in her face, Michaela replied, "Yes, madame."

"I know you go to school. We see you every afternoon."

Michaela looked at her unhappily. She is fearful, thought Julia. Perhaps she thinks we are curious about her being in this country because there may be something irregular about it. She said, "Next year I will not have to go to school. I can get a card of permission to work."

"But you are working now."

"Only to help my maman."

"Wouldn't it be better to go to school for a little longer — to be trained for something?"

The girl contemplated Laura for a long moment. Finally, turning back to the tea things, she replied, "There is nothing I can learn to do here."

When Michaela had gone, Julia said, "What do you suppose she meant by that? I suppose she could only be apprenticed to some trade that is carried on here in the village — there are no factories nearby."

For the following week Michaela came in the afternoon with the tea trolley. Julia noticed that Mme. Guerin — she supposed it must be Mme. Guerin who did so — provided a variety of small pastries, convinced, no doubt, that little bread and butter sandwiches and slices of Dundee cake must surely pall. Laura noticed these and one afternoon she said to Michaela before she could leave the room, "Wouldn't you like one of these?"

Michaela gazed at the little cream-filled puff held lightly in Laura's pink-tipped fingers and said eagerly, "Oh, yes, madame!" and plucked it up and popped it into her mouth.

Laura, delighted, laughed.

"Does Mme. Guerin make these?" Julia asked.

Michaela turned her eyes on Julia. "No, madame. They come from the patisserie in the village. I bring them up every afternoon."

When Michaela took away the trolley and closed the door, Julia said, "I'm really puzzled. She does speak English — or at least understands it — but it is obvious that French is her language. And if her mother is English, why aren't they in England? With Europe so overloaded with itinerants, why not be back where they can claim to be home?"

"There must be some reason. Perhaps it is her mother's decision — perhaps England would not be so comfortable for her."

"But why?"

Laura shook her head. "I don't know. But the girl deserves a better chance."

"And you think that you should provide it."

The next afternoon, when Michaela brought the tea trolley, there was a new variety of pastry on it. Michaela, as if she could not hold back, spoke before either of them greeted her. "Madame Julie, madame Laure, the patisserie has sent a novelty. It is a —" Michaela stopped and frowned. The young face, animated, suddenly showed the promise of the mature beauty that would some day be there. "It is something that is made in — where I come from. I do not know how to call it in French."

Her eyes shone with the pleasure she felt in offering it to them. Laura said, "Why, it looks delicious. And where do you come from Michaela?"

Michaela was instantly abashed, and dropped her eyes. "It is to the east."

Laura did not press her. When she had gone, savoring the novelty, Julia said, lifting a sugary morsel, "To the east. She could be Greek, Turkish —"

Laura added, "Or the Savoy in France. That is east of here." And they both laughed.

Laura poured the tea and they ate and drank in silence. Then Julia said, "We've never seen so much of the real Michaela before. Usually she just obeys when she is told to do something. There is a wall there to hide behind."

"And I want to find what is behind the wall."

"To change the metaphor, hidden fires burning out of sight. Of course, she feels like an outsider. She lives in a place that is not hers."

"And you add that to the fact that she is an adolescent. Teenage children nearly always feel as if they don't belong where they live. Didn't you feel a stranger to everything when you were that age?"

"I remember being pretty miserable, a lot of the time, anyway. Miserable because I didn't seem to fit in with the world I lived in, but I didn't know why. I always seemed to be putting my foot into something. All the other girls seemed to know how to handle their lives — how to deal with boys, how to deal with their mothers, how to deal with their mothers' friends, how to act socially. I was always either too shy or too aggressive and I suffered agonies over all the social errors I thought I committed. I was sure there was something wrong with me. I knew I didn't fit in, but it was only later that I understood why."

"Of course, you preferred girls to boys — and in time women to men. And certainly there wasn't anywhere for girls like you when you were Michaela's age."

"Well, the world is per se a dangerous place for girls, I'll give you that." Julia got up and crossed the room to the bathroom; their own bathroom was one of the amenities of their suite in Mme. Guerin's house. Presently she called out to Laura through the open door, "I didn't realize that we can see the back of the house next door from this window. There is a cobbled yard down there and the door in the wall where Michaela brings the groceries."

Laura came into the room and joined her at the window. She saw the cobbled space shaded by a gnarled old pear tree. Tufts of grass and weeds grew between the large stones. A battered watering can stood by the house door whose green paint was peeling. Laura said, "A scene for an Impressionist painter, untidy but full of subtle light and shadow."

"So it is. That must be the door Michaela uses when she comes over to Mme. Guerin's."

Thereafter Julia kept a watch on the patch of yard next door. Once or twice she saw Michaela's mother come out and hang clothes on a clothesline stretched across one corner. Once she saw Michaela arrive with her sack of groceries, which she placed on a wooden bench under the pear tree. Julia could hear the mother's strident voice call out from within the house. The poor girl, she thought; she treats her more like a slave than a daughter.

But then there was a morning when Julia looked out and saw the woman come out of the door, calling back to Michaela in her imperfect French, saying that she was going to Mme. Guerin's to help with preparations for a new group of guests and that Michaela must not forget to tidy the house and prepare the lunches for their own guests. It was Saturday, of course, Julia realized, and Michaela would not be going to school. Once the woman had vanished, the quiet scene below held Julia's eyes. Laura was right. Unkempt though it was, nevertheless it held the components that would catch a painter's eye, the blend of colors and shapes, the general composition of a painting.

As she mused she was suddenly aware that the little courtyard was no longer empty. Michaela had come out of the house door and was standing in the open space between the pear tree and the clothesline. She seemed to poise herself like — yes, like someone preparing to dance. Then she stretched forward one foot in its worn espadrille and moved it slowly first one way and then the other. Quickly she spun round on her other heel and began to bound about the small space in eager leaps, with her arms flung out. Laura's voice said in Julia's ear, "Why, it's the sketch of a ballet dancer's pirouette! She is imitating someone she has watched somewhere. So that is it. She wants to be a dancer."

They watched the girl. Even from a distance it was obvious that Michaela was wrapped up in what she was doing, that the stolid air of patient endurance with which she did everything else was obliterated by the ecstacy of dancing.

Julia said critically, "She is clumsy — and what

an awful terrain to dance on! But she has the right idea. She needs teaching."

"As in everything else," said Laura, gazing rapt at the whirling figure. "She is strong. You see that from the way she moves. She is clumsy because she has so much strength but does not know how to manage it. She can learn grace. Poor child."

"Yes, poor child. But she has a gift she can cultivate."

"But how will she do that? You remember she said that there was nothing taught here that she wanted to learn."

They both watched in silence for a while, watched as Michaela stood still and carefully placed her feet in what she evidently believed were the right positions.

Julia said, "Do you suppose her mother knows about this? Or does she do this on the sly, as now, while her mother is not around?"

"Her mother evidently expects that she is doing the housework. Look!"

Michaela suddenly stopped dancing and went into the house. In a moment she came out again and sat down on the bench, holding a basket of peas, which she began to shell, rapidly and with concentration.

"You have your answer there," said Laura. "She expects her mother to be back soon. Evidently her mother does not approve of wasting time."

Surprised by the tartness of her tone, Julia glanced at her. "You're a little hard on her. We don't know that she doesn't want Michaela to dance."

"There is something clandestine in the way she acts — as if she is enjoying stolen sweets — doing something her mother would not approve."

"Well, I suppose she is harassed by circumstances. Her establishment is a far cry from Mme. Guerin's and perhaps even so it's a failing enterprise. She doesn't seem the sort of woman who could make a success of any business venture — a failure before she begins."

They looked down again into the courtyard. Michaela was gathering up the bowl of peas and the basket of shells. In a moment she was gone, slipping through the house door, which she left open behind her.

Each day for several days they saw Michaela come out into the courtyard and dance, full of awkward movements but with an air of earnest striving. Inevitably she was interrupted by her mother's voice, irascible and impatient, calling her from within the house. Then one day they saw her come slowly out of the door and instead of leaping into a dance, she sat down on the bench. There was something resigned in the stance of her body, as if she was too weary, too discouraged to savor the free moments of ecstacy that dancing seemed to bring her.

"Oh, Julia!" Laura murmured into Julia's ear. "She's too young to give up!"

Julia, anxious to soothe Laura, said, "She's just tired. The poor kid works all the time."

The next afternoon it was not Michaela who brought the tea trolley but instead one of Mme. Guerin's maids. Michaela, she explained, was too busy helping her mother, who was overwhelmed by the flood of extra guests that Mme. Guerin could not accommodate. When the maid had gone Julia said, "Michaela's free moment was short-lived."

"Yes," said Laura, pouring the tea. "I am going to talk to Mme. Guerin about some sort of special schooling for Michaela — whether she thinks Michaela's mother has any idea of some sort of training for her."

Julia raised her eyebrows. "Perhaps you should be careful about getting too involved. We're going back to the States any day — at least, that is what I thought we had agreed."

Laura's tone was testy. "Yes, I know. But I can't walk away from this — I can't ignore the promise that seems to be waiting to flower there. Suppose it was quenched for want of a helping hand."

Julia made an impatient sound. "Darling, must you always succumb to these romantic impulses? Michaela is a sturdy girl, spiritually as well as physically, I think. She'll find her own way."

"But wouldn't it be gratifying to see what one could do to help?"

Julia sighed in resignation. "Yes, I'm sure it would gratify you."

In the morning, at the early hour when Mme. Guerin usually sat with them to drink coffee and eat a brioche in the deserted lounge — she had soon learned that they liked to be up and out for a walk before breakfast was served to them in their room — Laura brought up the subject of Michaela.

"There seems to be no future for the girl in her present circumstances," she said. "Does her mother have any plans for her?"

Mme. Guerin's eyebrows lifted and she replied in her most marked chatelaine's voice, "But, madame, what do you expect? You know, I'm sure, that

France is overrun these days by foreigners — indigents. We give them shelter from persecution wherever they come from. We offer them the benefits of our civilization. What more can we do — what more can we be expected to do —?"

"But, Mme. Guerin, I don't mean to criticize what you do. What I wonder is whether her mother has any plan for her daughter?"

The Frenchwoman shrugged. "What can she do? She has no means. I do not think her venture in running her pension is successful. I think that with the end of this season she will have to go elsewhere — perhaps on public assistance."

Julia, recognizing that Mme. Guerin was sensitive to the idea that French culture was being questioned, that it stood in danger of being drowned in the flood of indigent aliens, said hastily, "We are not criticizing your generosity, Mme. Guerin. We know you have been a good friend to this girl and her mother. That is not what Laura means. We are just wondering about Michaela's promise. She seems to have some special quality — something out of the ordinary — something that would respond to a little help." Good God, thought Julia, dismayed at her own words. I'm carrying this too far. Laura always seems to get me into these situations.

Mme. Guerin listened to her with fixed attention. Her shrewd eyes moved from Laura to Julia and back again. She asked, "You are interested in befriending her?"

"Well, yes," Laura answered, "within limits."

"Of course. One must be practical. I will admit that I have felt a certain sympathy for the girl. It is

31

troubling to see a young life badly affected by bad circumstances — and especially in the world we know today."

"The point is," Laura persisted, "do you think that her mother would welcome the idea of Michaela's being given a chance for a better education — for training of some sort —"

There was speculation in Mme. Guerin's eyes. "I think it is possible that the girl might have gifts for training in some art or craft. She is by nature a bohemian, but that is not proper for a young girl and her mother certainly would object. Madame Souza is — how do you say? — narrow in her outlook — commendably so, since she is responsible for the girl's morals."

"What do you mean, madame?"

"I think perhaps Michaela has talent for the stage, as an entertainer. But that is not a life for a young girl."

"Exactly," said Laura, eagerly. "She does have a talent."

Mme. Guerin looked at her shrewdly. "You have observed something, madame?"

"Yes," said Laura.

Julia added quickly, "I think the girl wants to be a dancer."

"Ah! So you have seen — what I have seen," said Mme. Guerin. "She is a little old to begin that career."

"But if she has a special gift —?" said Laura.

Mme. Guerin said skeptically, "She has the desire. But does she have the gift? Who can say?"

"But she should have the chance."

Mme. Guerin looked at Laura from under her eyebrows. "You are determined, I see. What do you propose?"

Julia looked at Laura. Her glance said, "Do we propose anything?"

Laura said to Mme. Guerin, "Do you know whether Michaela's mother knows of her daughter's ambition?"

Mme. Guerin said crisply, "I know nothing. I merely observe."

"Well, could you talk to her — she must be ready to listen to any suggestion you might make."

Mme. Guerin inclined her head. "Yes. I think so. I shall proceed carefully."

A couple of days later, when they came in from a visit to the village, Mme. Guerin beckoned them into her office. She would be brief, she said, since she had much to do to prepare for the influx of weekend guests who were expected. She had consulted Mme. Souza. Yes, Mme. Souza knew of Michaela's infatuation with ballet. Where they had been before coming here — probably some large city, probably Paris — Michaela had observed ballet dancers. It was a foolish notion, some childish fancy. But she was not averse to hearing what the ladies might have to say about providing some sort of training for Michaela.

"It was left there, mesdames. I thought I had better let you know that much, before you proceed further. And now —" Mme. Guerin began to bustle about the room, and Julia and Laura left her.

In their own sitting room Julia said, "And what are you going to do now?"

Laura was silent for a while. Finally she asked, "Would you consider taking her with us back to New York?"

Only half surprised Julia said, "Yes. But I don't know how it is to be done. There are immigration laws, you know. There are such things as student visas. I should have to sponsor her."

"But you would."

"If you put it that way, I don't see how I can refuse."

Laura's anxious seriousness broke down into a laugh. "Oh, Julia! We must go and call on Mme. Souza. We must get off on the right foot."

They approached the front door of the house. The entrance was further down the hill. There was a sense of crossing a boundary as they walked up the unkempt drive, a boundary that marked the difference between the spruceness of Mme. Guerin's establishment and the shabbiness of her neighbor. Voicing this, Laura said, "Of course, these are old houses. It must take a great deal of care to keep them up."

Julia agreed. "It takes someone like Mme. Guerin to provide the polish. A lesser spirit cannot cope."

As they reached the front door it was opened and Mme. Souza stood inside, gesturing for them to come in. Julia thought, evidently she has been waiting for us. She spoke their names and invited them to follow her down a long dark corridor to a room that looked out on the courtyard where they had seen Michaela.

Seen at close range the impression she had made

at a distance was confirmed. A woman about my age, forty, that is, Laura guessed, with faded blond hair and fair skin that had lost its freshness. The room was furnished with old-fashioned furniture. A tea table was set near the window — a proper English tea, Julia noticed, without the French fancies that Mme. Guerin provided. They sat down and she served them tea. They spoke of the weather, the fine summer, the approach of the end of the season. Then they sat holding their tea cups in silence.

Eventually Mme. Souza said, "Mme. Guerin has told me that you want to speak to me about Michaela."

"Yes," said Laura. "We like Michaela very much. We should like to help her."

"Help her? How?" The sharp questions were full of suspicion.

"It seems a pity that a girl like Michaela should not have a chance to learn something she wants to do."

There was an angry look in Mme. Souza's eyes. "I cannot pay for special lessons for her. I have no means. I cannot stay here. This venture is not a success. I must give up this house at the end of the year."

"Perhaps you should go back to England."

"Back to England? No, that was all over too long ago."

In the short silence that followed Julia looked covertly from Mme. Souza to Laura. Undoubtedly they understood each other instinctively; Julia was often struck by the quickness with which English people evaluated each other's social status. Also, she saw that Laura and Mme. Souza did not like each other.

"You mean you no longer have relations there who might help you."

"I have no connections left there."

"But after all, it is your home."

"It is not home to me any longer." Mme. Souza spoke with bitter finality and her face had taken on a stony expression.

"Still, you must provide for yourself and Michaela."

"Yes. The girl is a worry to me. If it were just myself, I would have no problem. But I cannot take her back to England. She would not fit in. It is hard to teach her to do anything properly. She is careless and moons about."

Julia said, "Isn't that her age? Aren't most girls her age careless and given to daydreaming?"

Mme. Souza agreed impatiently.

Laura asked, "Is she disobedient?"

"Oh, no. She obeys."

"Then she is teachable. Perhaps she has a talent that can be developed."

Mme. Souza looked at her blankly. "What do you mean?"

"Laura and I have noticed — and Mme. Guerin says she has, too — that Michaela likes to dance. Mme. Guerin thinks perhaps Michaela can become a dancer."

Mme. Souza said quickly, "Mme. Guerin has said nothing to me about such a thing. She has not told me what you wanted to talk to me about in regard to Michaela."

"Perhaps," Laura interjected, "we should ask Michaela some questions."

"I must know what you want to ask before I call her," Mme. Souza declared adamantly.

Julia said, "We think that perhaps we could provide for Michaela, if she does indeed have a talent for dancing. There are schools that train girls as dancers."

"Such places are not respectable."

"Some of them are."

"I cannot afford to live in Paris. I cannot find work there."

Julia contemplated her for a moment. "Would you allow us to take her back to New York with us? There are good dancing schools there."

"Oh, no. I could not let her go so far away without me. She is too young."

But Julia had noticed that in her refusal a note of calculation had crept in. "She would be under our care."

Mme. Souza was silent for a moment. "I cannot leave here right now. I have a lease on this house till the end of the year. It would take me time to wind things up."

So, thought Julia, we're taking you too.

Laura interjected, "But still, we must talk to Michaela."

Mme. Souza got up abruptly and said, "I will call her," and walked out of the room.

Laura said, "She has been very well trained as

someone's housekeeper. I'm sure of that. She is right. She would have no trouble providing for herself. But Michaela —?"

Julia said ruefully, "I seem to have got us in pretty deep."

Laura smiled at her. "Yes, darling. I can always count on you."

She raised her hand at a sound outside the room. Mme. Souza came back in. Michaela, wearing the white blouse and blue jumper of her school uniform, followed her in and stood in the middle of the room as her mother sat down. She looked at the floor and did not speak.

"Michaela," said Laura in a gentle voice, "you like to dance, don't you?"

Michaela's head came up in a jerk. "Oh, yes, madame!"

"Would you like to learn properly?"

"Oh, yes, madame!" Michaela spoke eagerly and then glanced guiltily at her mother. There was no change of expression in Mme. Souza's face.

"Would you like to come to New York with us and go to school?"

Mme. Souza frowned, but Laura went on quickly, "You understand, this is a very serious matter. We must be sure you really want to do this — that if we arrange for you to learn, you must stick to it."

Michaela, under Laura's serious gaze, blushed and stammered, "Oh, madame —" and could not go on but dropped her eyes again in silence.

Julia said to Mme. Souza, "There are a lot of things that would have to be done — a lot of inquiries we must make. I am sure you understand that. But, first, we must have your consent."

"Yes," said Mme. Souza.

"We'll let you know if we find that what we want to do is feasible," said Julia, getting up.

As they walked back to the Auberge Celestin, Julia said, "It was the mention of New York that did it. She sees this as an opportunity for herself."

"Yes," said Laura, preoccupied. "I'm going to have another interview with her."

"What about?" Julia demanded.

"About herself."

The next morning Laura announced after breakfast that she was going to visit Mme. Souza. Michaela, she said, would be in school, and the way would be clear for a talk with her mother. Julia, aware that Laura had spent a restless night and needed to settle some question in her own mind, did not demur. She watched Laura walk across to the house next door.

She was gone a long time. When at last she came back she was absentminded and for a while silent.

Julia, impatient, said, "Well, what is it?"

Laura said, "I decided that, if we are going to make ourselves responsible for Michaela, I had better know more about her mother."

To fill the pause that followed this statement, Julia said, "Not a bad idea."

Laura continued in silence, lost in recollection. Finally, she began, "Her name was originally Daphne Collins. She is my age. She comes from the Midlands. When she left school she went to London and eventually she went to Portugal as a nursery governess for an English businessman's family, who lived there. She was seduced by a man who was a servant in their house. At least, she says that this was what her employers believed: an inexperienced young woman in a strange society who became infatuated by a man who took advantage of her infatuation. But she says that this was not really the case. It was a genuine romance, she says; she was not a dupe. When she became pregnant, her employers brought pressure to bear on him to make him marry her. Again, that was their view. She says he was perfectly willing to marry her. But after the child was born and she had lived with his family for a year or so, she could stand it no longer; she had left her employers, of course. There was too big a gap between what she was used to and their customs. I suspect that, though he was a Portuguese national, he came from elsewhere. I could not get her to tell me what he really was; perhaps a gypsy, sure enough. She insisted on having her own place, even if it was a single room in a tenement. Shortly after that he left, without warning. She suspects that he went to Germany as a guest worker; it was during the labor shortage in the seventies. She never heard from him again. My own thought is that he could no longer put up with her demands for him to conform to her idea of respectability. She came to France after that and has lived a hand-to-mouth existence since — but perfectly respectably, she assures me. I believe her, because it is terribly important to her that she should be seen as a properly married woman with a legitimate child and a proper way of living. She did not consider going back to England because she could not face the thought of explaining her failed marriage and the odd child she had produced."

"But she did not consider abandoning Michaela, either, did she?"

"Oh, no! Michaela is hers, no matter how strange and incomprehensible to her. What she wants now is security — financial and social security."

Julia pondered. "I think she also sees Michaela as a means to achieving that."

"Perhaps you are right," said Laura.

* * * * *

At last they had all the arrangements made and the official documents obtained. Michaela would travel with them to New York. Her mother would stay behind, finishing the season. She would come to join Michaela whenever she could wind up her business affairs. Julia would provide her plane fare. The alacrity with which she agreed to all this prompted Julia to say to Laura that it was obvious that Mme. Souza knew how to take advantage of circumstances. Mme. Guerin, overhearing the remark, smiled and said, after all, if one must live by one's wits, one must learn to seize opportunities.

"But you understand, dear," Julia said to Laura, "I'm going to have to spend a few days in New York before I can go down with you to Virginia."

"Well, then," said Laura promptly, "we'll send Michaela down to stay with the Houghtons until we get there. That will give you time to deal with your affairs. I am sure I can find someone I know who can take her to Washington and put her on the bus for Sutford. My father-in-law can meet her there when she gets off the bus. I have told them that we shall spend a little while with them until you must get back to the University."

II

Though the traces of summer still lingered, the prospect of autumn was in the Virginia countryside. Julia, driving the car along the gently winding road, saw the first signs — a gum tree with a few red leaves, a field stripped of its summer crop. The rolling hills were still green against the purple-brown backdrop of the Blue Ridge. Laura, sitting beside her, watched for the signposts that had become familiar to her in previous visits.

Around another curve in the road they found

they were in the outskirts of Sutford, a small town whose main street was lined with large houses set back behind wide lawns. A few minutes more and they were in the center of the town. The lawns had disappeared and the street was lined with small brick buildings occupied by stores, a church, a gas station, a bank. Standing at the only traffic light Julia saw the placard fixed to a lamppost. It announced a play at the Barn Theater, with a photograph of a scene on stage and the names of actors and the times of performances. It was dated in the past August.

Julia pointed to it.

Laura, following her gesture, said, "That's Mrs. Outhwaite's theater. I've heard she had a very good season."

A little further along they saw some more placards, tattered and blowing in the light wind. These advertised a ballet troupe which was coming to finish the season at the Barn Theater with a performance of a Balanchine fragment.

Julia said, "Does she have ballet also?"

"That is something new," said Laura.

They drove on until they were beyond the further limit of the town and then Laura indicated a road that branched off to the right. Here the houses were more widely spaced, with large grounds and meadows beyond, in some of which horses stood.

Presently Laura said, "This is the turn-off. The Houghtons' place is the first we'll come to. Beyond that the road goes on to the farm. Half way along on the left is the lane to Margot Outhwaite's house."

As she turned into the narrow road Julia said, "Then this is a private road."

"Well, it is in a sense. It does not go beyond the farm."

"The farm?"

"The Houghtons' farm. They have a tenant who manages it."

"The Barn Theater is at Mrs. Outhwaite's?"

"Yes. In fact, it is the old barn. Her house — it is called The Shrubberies because of the old boxwood surrounding it — was once a farm. It is ancient, quite a monument in these parts."

The winding road took them steadily up through rolling hills. Sometimes the bushes beside the road were high enough to cut off the view and sometimes they flattened so that there were vistas of broad farmlands and wide meadows with clusters of cows gathered under the occasional great oak or maple.

"Wasn't Mrs. Outhwaite well-known at one time — in the theater?"

"Oh, yes! Years ago. She's 80 now. She produced plays after she gave up acting. I understand she still takes a small part occasionally in the plays she puts on."

"It's strange that she should come and live so out of the world now."

"It is not so much so as you would think. Her summer theater brings crowds down here, from Washington, from New York. I'm surprised you don't know about it."

"My attention has been otherwise engaged," said Julia primly. "You forget I've spent every available moment on the other side of the Atlantic with someone I could name but won't."

Laura laughed. "Well, she's been doing this for the last ten years. People come from everywhere to visit her."

"She must have money."

"Some, I suppose. And she is good at getting financial support for her enterprises from people who have a great deal more."

"You know her, of course."

"I've never met her. She has always been away when I've been visiting here. She is a friend of Mother Houghton's. She bought The Shrubberies ten years ago and it is surprising what good friends they have become — they are such dissimilar women."

"Opposites attract, they say — like you and me."

"Are we so opposite?"

Julia did not reply. They had reached the driveway that led up to a large brick house. Julia drove up to the graveled space in front of the wide white doorway. It was a two-storied house in its middle portion with one-storied wings on the sides. A woman was standing at the top of the flight of shallow steps, the front door open behind her.

As soon as the car came to a stop Laura jumped out and ran up the steps to embrace her. Dick's mother, thought Julia, getting out of the car more slowly. In spite of the fifteen years that she and Laura had maintained their relationship back and forth across the ocean she had never met the older Houghtons, by chance or by Laura's design, she was not quite sure.

When she reached the top step Laura, standing with one arm around her mother-in-law's waist, said,

"Dear, this is my friend Julia. I've spoken about her to you often."

Mrs. Houghton's manner was reserved. Female university professors, thought Julia, probably are rather out of her usual circle. She was a spare woman, the same height as Laura, with white hair carefully dressed, as if she had been recently to the beauty parlor. She wore a flowered summer dress and a cardigan. There was a twinkle about her of necklace, rings and eyeglasses.

Still gazing fixedly at her, Mrs. Houghton said, "You're very welcome. Any friend of Laura's is especially welcome in this house. My husband is not here at the moment. He is in town. Please come in. I'll send the girl to fetch your bags."

They entered the dusky hallway, lit only by the brilliance that came in through the doorway. A stairway rose at one side and the door to the living room was open at the other. An old house, thought Julia, as they walked into the big room filled with old-fashioned furniture. She felt ill-at-ease because she was aware that Mrs. Houghton's poise was tremulously insecure, that if Laura had arrived alone, she would have clung to her in a far more emotional welcome. In an effort to relieve some of this well-bred restraint, Julia walked to the big window and gazed out at the garden, laid out in a formal pattern of pebbled walks and tidy flower beds.

Behind her she heard Mrs. Houghton's tearful murmuring and Laura's gentle voice trying to soothe. She heard little snatches of talk, Mrs. Houghton's voice obviously muffled as she pressed her face into Laura's shoulder. "It has seemed so long, Laura

47

dear. I've ached to have you here. I can't believe that Dick is gone for good. His father gets impatient with me, but there is no use my pretending. It is only to you that I can open my heart, only you can understand what I feel."

Good God! Julia silently protested. Oh Laura. She knew that Dick had been the only child of middle-aged parents — the cherished prodigy. Over the years she had learned from Laura the extent to which their pride in him had grown, the anxiety with which she had worked to prevent them from knowing the true nature of his character and exploits. Dick was the world-renowned reporter, the man thousands, millions of people, had come to look to on TV for information about the great events in the world. He was brilliant, courageous, ready to go anywhere where news was to be made. What his private exploits were they did not know.

The murmurs from the other end of the room grew quieter. Julia turned away from the window and walked back to where the other women sat.

Laura was saying, "But where is Michaela?"

Mrs. Houghton said, visibly surprised, as if she had forgotten Michaela, "Why, she is with Margot — Mrs. Outhwaite. She is an odd girl. She acts as if she was not used to speaking English or being spoken to in English. Yet I understand that her mother is English. I suppose that comes from living in France so long. Oh, no, she had no trouble getting here on the bus. Fred met her at the depot. I expect she is used to looking after herself."

"But why is she with Mrs. Outhwaite now? Didn't she know we were coming today?"

"Oh, she has been staying with Margot. I didn't

know what to do with her here. Margot said she'd look after her. She could help Orinda around the house. Margot is quite taken with her. But then Margot has been in the theater, you know, and she is used to all kinds of people."

"Then we'll not see her this evening."

"Well, no. Of course, when Fred comes I could ask him to go and fetch her —"

There was obvious reluctance in her voice and Laura said hastily, "Oh, no, no! We'll see her tomorrow."

There was the sound of tires on the gravel outside and presently Fred Houghton came in — a tall man with nearly-white hair and a grizzled moustache. He greeted Laura as if she was in fact his daughter. He gave Julia a piercing look out of shrewd blue eyes, as if he was checking this first sight of her against what he had heard of her beforehand. Julia was relieved that the conversation was confined to the topic of their — hers and Laura's — trip from New York, the condition of the weather and what they might expect for tomorrow.

Then Mrs. Houghton suggested that they might like to go to their room before dinner was served. "You must be tired," she said, "and would like to refresh yourselves."

Julia followed Laura up the wide stairs to the upper landing and into the large room in the front corner of the house. She was surprised at the sight of the four-poster double bed, covered with an heirloom quilt. She looked at Laura who smiled.

"How did you manage that? When she said 'room' I thought it meant at least twin beds."

Laura laughed. "I doubt if there are any twin

49

beds in this house. There is only one other spare bedroom, the one at the back of the house. It was Dick's when he was growing up. She has kept it just as he left it when he went away to college. I know that she is very reluctant to use it for anybody else. So I said we'd be very comfortable here — where I always sleep when I come to visit."

There were drinks before dinner and a brief period in the living room after. While Laura and Mrs. Houghton murmured together, Fred Houghton sat down on the sofa next to Julia. He began to talk about the problems of the farm which was still part of his property. He had spent the afternoon with his tenant, he said, a reliable man but one without much enterprise when it came to trying new methods.

"Not like that boy of his. Chris is still in high school but I think he'll turn out to be quite a fellow. He deserves a good education."

Aware that his intent was to establish friendship with her and that this conversation was the means to that end, Julia responded as well as she could. From the problems of his own farm he went on to talk about agriculture in the state of Virginia generally. Julia gathered that he had a great deal to do with local politics and that this interest was something that went back among the Houghtons to former generations. While he talked Julia studied the large dark portrait over the mantel of a gentleman clad in the dark coat and white stock of the years before the Civil War. No doubt, he, too, had had much to do with local public affairs.

Then Mrs. Houghton, who went to bed early, said

that perhaps they would like to retire to recover from their long drive.

Settled into the double bed, Julia said, "She really clings to you. But you've misled her all these years about what Dick was really like as a husband."

"She would never have believed anything else. And she has always been fond of me. How could I try to disillusion her?"

"How to tell her that he was a miserable husband — no husband at all, in fact — a philanderer who willingly spent as much of his time away from you as he wanted — not the dedicated man of public service who paid this price for principle? And you the faithful wife — Penelope to Odysseus. How many times did you get the clap from him? And the only reason you haven't got AIDS is because you stopped sleeping with him ten years ago."

"Don't go on like that, Julia! I can't stand it! Don't you know how I chastise myself for the waste of all these years? But still I don't think I could have done otherwise. I was committed to him and then it became a sort of public character for me, didn't it? What sort of a wreck would it have made of me and them to do otherwise?"

"But you should stop now. You shouldn't let her go on draining you as a relief for her own grief."

"No, I am not going to do that. But I must act slowly. You must remember that she does not know the whole story. Nobody does, except you and me — and Catharine. And Catharine does not know that you do."

"But Catharine was only the last episode. He had

been finding and discarding women all the time you were married to him. And coming back each time to cajole you into picking up with him where you had left off, as if nothing had happened. And, more fool you, you always did."

"It was for the same reason that he was always traveling the world. He was too restless for anything else. Before I met you, dear, I used to agonize over it — my hollow marriage. But I had committed myself and I had found out that he was a frightened man — frightened in ways nobody but I ever found out. He was always trying to prove he was what he wasn't and then I was always trying to help him understand that he was afraid of — ghosts. He just didn't feel he was up to what was expected of him so he strove to prove, to himself, that he was. You know, I think it was his father who made him feel inadequate. He wasn't the son his father wanted. But when I met you, I saw that I was playing a losing game. It was a great liberation for me, dear, when I met you. I saw everything then as it really was."

"But you wouldn't break with him and come with me."

"It was too late. I couldn't do it. He thought by then I would always be there when he came back. His parents thought he had an ideal marriage with an ideal wife — a wife who supported him in all the great things he did and wanted to do. Oh, Julia —"

Laura buried her face in Julia's neck. Julia said, "Commitments can be nullified by the emergence of truth."

"Perhaps I was coming around to that when he discovered he had AIDS. It was impossible after that. You know this. But you needn't have stayed with me."

Julia said bitterly, "You know I didn't have an option. How could I walk away from the most important part of my life? But here we are dangling."

Laura rose up on her elbow and threw herself on top of Julia. She pinned Julia's head between her arms. "Must you keep at me? I won't have it! I've got to tie up the strings properly. I won't live with a remnant of guilt getting in the way between us. I want to be free to love you openly the way I've always loved you in secret. I want to be free, free of these clinging hands —"

She subsided onto Julia and Julia held her close. "Hush," she said. "All right, we're committed to seeing this through. So I won't say anything more."

They were quiet for a while till Julia felt Laura's body grow soft and clinging. Then she said, "Have you heard anything from Catharine?"

"No, but Mother Houghton has. She asked me who Catharine was. She showed me a letter she had received from her some weeks ago. Catharine said in it that she was so sorry to hear of Dick's death. What astonished Mother Houghton was that she asked for some little memento of him — some small object of no great value, something identified with him."

"What did you say?"

"I said that I knew Catharine, that she is a well-known reporter on one of the big TV networks — the Houghtons never look at TV now that Dick is dead — and that she had known Dick for a long time — which wasn't exactly true but it made it sound more plausible. I reminded her of how popular Dick had always been, how many people knew and admired him, people who wrote to him from all over the world, telling him how much they depended on the news he reported about great events — wars, catastrophes, assassinations — since he was always in the thick of things."

"What did she say to that?"

"She wondered why Catharine did not ask me for a memento. She wondered how Catharine knew where she lived. I told her that it was easy enough to find that out. So then she said she supposed it wouldn't hurt to respond to Catharine's request. Did I have something to send her?"

"Do you?"

"Of course. He had a keyring with an oriental design on it. I don't know where he got it but he never was without it. It was a sort of talisman. He never lost it, though he lost most of his personal belongings over and over again when he traveled. He was very careless about possessions. But he never lost that. He said it was solid brass made from a bit of cannon used in the Napoleonic wars and the design had some reference to Napoleon's Egyptian campaign."

"Do you care about it?"

"No. I don't want reminders of that sort. It is among the things in the London flat. I told Mother Houghton I would send it to Catharine when I got back there — whenever that is going to be."

Laura sighed as she sank down once more beside Julia, welcoming her kisses as a prelude to love.

* * * * *

The next morning, when they went downstairs, they found the breakfast room — a small room at the side of the house with many windows to let in the early sun — filled with light. Mrs. Houghton sat at the table by herself. Her husband, she said, had already gone on up to the farm.

"We keep country hours. Will you have an egg, Laura? And you, Julia?" She gestured towards an egg poacher on an electric grill on the sideboard. As Laura got up to attend to the eggs, she said to Julia, "As you see, we don't have all the modern conveniences. But we're accustomed to things as they are and at our age we do not have the urge to change. You don't, you know, when you don't have young people to spur you on. It has always been a sorrow to us that our son did not have a family." She glanced toward Laura as she said this, as if to absolve her from blame.

If Laura heard this, she did not show it. She placed a lightly poached egg in front of Julia and sat down with her own.

Laura said, "I'm sorry you found Michaela troublesome."

"Oh, she was not troublesome. It was just that I am not used to having a young person like that about and she seemed so difficult to communicate with. Dilsy got flustered with her in the kitchen. Margot comes over to see me almost every day. She noticed that things were not going well, so she said she would take the girl over to stay with her. You don't mind, do you, Laura?" she asked anxiously.

Julia saw that Laura did mind, but Laura said smoothly, "Oh, no, I shouldn't want to upset you.

But Mrs. Outhwaite — she is Margot? — I've never met her when I've been here before. She was once an actress, wasn't she? I didn't think she was a dancer."

Mrs. Houghton looked nonplussed. "Why, yes, she was an actress. Why would you suppose she was a dancer?"

"Doesn't she have some interest in dancing?" Laura persisted.

Julia interrupted, "We saw some old posters still up when we drove down here. One of them said there was a ballet to be performed at the Barn Theater."

"Well, yes. I believe she did have a troupe of dancers here at one time. We have so many visitors here on weekends in the summer. Margot has so many people who come for the shows she puts on. I do not pay much attention, unless she needs me to help her entertain, now and again. Everything she puts on is very popular. She has a wonderful way with these things." Mrs. Houghton paused and looked at Laura. "Is Michaela a dancer?"

"Not yet," said Laura. "She wants to be one. She needs to find out if she has the necessary talent."

"Well, perhaps Margot can help you. I think you said that her mother was coming from France later. Is Michaela like her? I cannot imagine anyone less English-looking."

"No. Mrs. Souza is quite different. In fact, she looks more like me," said Laura with a quick smile.

"Then she must have married someone very foreign-looking. Is she coming here? I don't really think I could manage with her."

"Oh, no. She is coming later, to stay with us in

New York. Julia and I want to give Michaela a chance to have a better life. She and her mother have had a very bad time just trying to live. You know, the world, especially Europe, is full of displaced people these days."

"Yes, I read about these things in newspapers. We seem to have our share of homeless people in this country. But, Laura dear, I know you have a very kind heart and you do so much to help unfortunate people. But this must be quite an outlay. I hope you will not regret your generosity."

"Oh, I've no need to pinch and save. Dick's affairs are being settled quite satisfactorily and I have my own income. Besides, Julia is sharing the expense."

"I am glad of that. I would have expected Dick to make proper provision for you." Mrs. Houghton did not see the glance that passed between Julia and Laura. "However, quite often people who benefit by such openhandedness as yours grow demanding. I've observed this in the past."

"I shall beware," Laura promised cheerfully. "But how do you suggest we go about finding Michaela? Does Mrs. Outhwaite have a daily routine? We don't want to intrude."

"She is unconventional and she does usually come over to chat with me during the day. But perhaps it would be best if you were to phone her. Her number is on the list I keep by the telephone. She knows you were to arrive yesterday."

When Laura dialed the number the phone rang for a long time before a high-pitched female voice said Hello. It took Laura several tries before she succeeded in identifying herself as Mrs. Houghton's daughter-in-law. At last she did succeed and added, "I understand Michaela is staying with you. May I come over with Julia to see her?"

"Michaela?" said the voice. "Oh, yes, she is here. Oh, I understand now! You're Dick Houghton's wife — widow, I should say. Such a sad loss for the Houghtons, especially when they were not able to be with him in his last illness. It was such a terrible journey for his mother, to go to England under those circumstances and Fred would not leave her. I understand he was too weak to travel. At least, that was the excuse he gave them. I know that people that are seriously ill often become very selfish — a natural human failing, I suppose."

Laura waited for her to come to a pause in the flow of words. Julia, sitting on the stairs watching her, saw pain and distress cross her face. Finally Laura was able to say into the phone, "I really must see Michaela, Mrs. Outhwaite. Now? Thank you. We'll be there in a few minutes. Yes, my friend Julia is with me. She is equally interested in Michaela. We shall see you soon, then."

Laura put the phone down and sat for a moment gazing at it absentmindedly.

"What did she say?" Julia demanded.

Laura looked nervously around. The phone was in the entrance hall, outside the breakfast room. She made a gesture to Julia and said in a purposely casual tone, "She expects us to come over now. I shall let Mother Houghton know."

In the car, as Julia backed out of the parking space, Laura said, "She thinks it was terrible that Dick did not make an effort to see his parents when he knew he was dying. But did he know? I don't think he wanted to admit that to himself. And how was I to let them know that the pneumonia he died of was only the last problem he had, the final breakdown? You know how hard I worked to keep the truth about his condition out of the news, out of the gossip columns. It was kidney failure, officially."

"Yes, yes," said Julia anxiously, turning the car into the narrow road that led to the farm. "This is the right way, isn't it? You know you don't have to justify yourself to me."

The distance to the opening of the lane that led to Mrs. Outhwaite's house was not great but the road was a narrow, high-crowned road that wound between high banks that only occasionally allowed glimpses of meadows and corn fields. There were signs posted frequently along the way buying that the Barn Theater was ahead — to lead the many strangers who came in the summertime, Julia supposed. Finally there was one that said, "You are here! Welcome to the old Barn," and Julia turned the car into the lane that led shortly into a wide graveled space in front of a huge red barn. Beyond, a piece of open land had been converted into a parking area, now deserted. The house was off to one side, hidden behind great ancient boxwoods, through which there was a narrow path, just wide enough for the car. They arrived at the front door of the old house, lying low amongst its shrubbery. An ancient oak tree shaded the entrance.

They got out of the car and stood looking about.

"What do we do now?" said Julia. "There doesn't seem to be anybody about."

"We could try the knocker." Laura pointed to the brightly polished brass knocker in the center of the red-painted door.

Julia raised the knocker and let it fall against the wood. They could hear the muffled boom from inside the house. But the sound died away and the silence returned. Julia stepped away from the door and walked toward one corner of the house to peer down the foot path that led through the hedge. At first she saw no one but then she exclaimed, "Michaela!"

As she spoke the girl ran down the path towards her. "Madame Julie! How happy I am to see you! Where is madame Laure? It has been such a long time!"

"Only a week," said Laura, coming to join Julia. Amusement and happiness showed in her eyes as she looked at Michaela, whose black eyes sparkled and whose cheeks, usually so sallow, had flushed red. She was wearing blue jeans — where did she get them, Julia wondered; Mrs. Outhwaite must have provided them — and a checked cotton shirt. Her abundant black hair was caught back with a broad red ribbon. She stood still, looking from one to the other of them. Laura stepped close and put her arm around her. "We're very glad to see you, too, Michaela. Where is Mrs. Outhwaite?"

"Madame Outhwaite —" There was a slight difficulty with the th — "is on the telephone. She is often on the telephone. People call her and she has much to say. But she is expecting you. So won't you come in?"

Michaela went to the front door and opened it; it

was not locked. She stood aside and waited for them to enter.

The vestibule was dusky and after the bright sunlight outside they found it hard to see the furnishings. Presently it was apparent that the old house was full of antiques — tables and chairs, lamps dating from a century ago, and pieces of statuary standing in the corners. The living room was long and low-ceilinged. Michaela, her fund of conversation exhausted, made a gesture towards the empire sofa indicating that they should sit down. Then she disappeared through the door at the far end of the room. Laura sat down on the sofa. Julia walked to the nearest long window and looked out into the garden that was surrounded by the boxwood. She said, "This must be older than the Houghtons' place."

"Yes, it is," said Laura. "I believe it goes back a long way. It was dilapidated when Mrs. Outhwaite took it over, according to the Houghtons. It used to have a farm surrounding it but now the fields belong to the Houghtons."

In the quiet they could hear the same high-pitched voice that had spoken to them on the phone, engaged in conversation somewhere close by. Presently the voice stopped and they heard the quick patter of high-heeled shoes on wooden floors. Mrs. Outhwaite burst into the room, exclaiming, "I'm so sorry to keep you waiting! But I am at the mercy of the telephone. It is the penalty for living at such a distance from the center of things. Everyone must reach me by phone. They can't simply drop by. I miss seeing people and talking face to face — there is a certain warmth in such contact. But then there are compensations. In the summer, of course, it is a different matter. There is always a crowd here."

As her stream of words engulfed them, Julia scrutinized her. She was an elderly woman, of average height, not plump but with the soft flesh of old age, overflowing with energy. The same age as Mrs. Houghton, probably, thought Julia — 80 more or less. Wisps of white hair escaped from under the wide-brimmed straw hat she wore. Evidently she had been outside in the garden when called to the phone. She still held muddy garden gloves in her hand.

She broke off what she was saying to ask, "Now which of you is Laura Houghton? It must be you." She turned to Laura as she spoke. "I should have known you at once by your English looks. How do you do, my dear? And you're Dr. Cochrane? Elizabethan literature is your field, isn't it? You know, we've never attempted Shakespeare. But I think perhaps we shall."

She talked for a while about the theater, about experimental theater, about her attempts to give an airing to new plays by unknown young playwrights, about the problems of putting on theatrical productions so far from the source, by which she meant New York. But presently she broke off and said, "But I am running on too long. I so enjoy an attentive audience. You've come to see Michaela. I expect that Eula" — Julia guessed that she was speaking of Mrs. Houghton by her given name — "has told you that she found it rather difficult to look after her, so I suggested that Michaela come and stay with me."

Laura said, "I'm sorry that she has caused a problem. I didn't think she would."

"Oh, I don't say she is a problem! It is simply that Eula is such a valetudinarian. I like to have young people around. It seems to postpone mortality — or at least the contemplation of it. Michaela is a very good girl, tries her best to be helpful though perhaps she does not always succeed. She is not used to our ways." Mrs. Outhwaite paused and looked at Laura speculatively. "Is she a gypsy?"

"Not that I know of," said Laura. "Her mother is English."

"That is what I thought Eula said. We were both astonished when she arrived. She is a very different type — very vivid. Perhaps her father —?"

"I've no idea," said Laura. "I do not know her mother very well. Certainly Michaela does not take after her."

"Well, I like having her here, though I must say that she is something of a problem for Orinda." Seeing the question in their faces she explained, "Orinda is my mainstay. She is a most important member of this establishment and I would never have anyone here who really annoyed her. But she is used to putting up with strangers. She is simply disconcerted by Michaela every so often. The girl does not seem to have any knack for household matters."

The echo of Mme. Guerin, thought Julia.

"We shan't be here very long," said Laura, "and of course we'll take Michaela back to New York with us."

"Oh, I'm not anxious for her to leave. She is not articulate — that is, in words. She has a more subtle way of conveying emotion. You've noticed that, I'm sure. She fascinates me. She has the essence of a good actress. She can convey things to you without you even being aware that she is doing so — till afterwards, when you come to think about it."

"Actress?" Laura queried. "I hadn't thought of her in that way."

"Then you see her more as a child of nature, perhaps."

"You think there is something there beyond what we see?"

"You must have sensed that there is something unusual about the girl — some promise — or you would not have undertaken to bring her home with you. The first thing she said to me — beyond the commonplaces — was to ask me about the ballet troupe we had here this summer —"

"We saw the posters for it still up in the town," said Julia.

"Ah, yes, they should be taken down. She asked me many questions about the dancers. The dance troupe was the last performance we had this summer. It was an innovation. I'm afraid I neglect Eula during the season. I don't get over to see her as often as I should. After the troupe left I was busy winding things up here. So I was somewhat out-of-date with current events when I did go to see her and she told me that you were sending Michaela to stay with her for a few days. I gathered that you had found her somewhere where you had been abroad — that you were rescuing her from bad circumstances."

"Not exactly bad circumstances," said Laura. "Julia and I came across her in a French town where we were staying. Her mother was trying to run a pension, not very successfully. They are not French nationals so their difficulties were compounded. We discovered that Michaela wants to be a dancer."

"Ah!" Mrs. Outhwaite exclaimed. "So that's it! In any case, it struck me that Michaela was rather upsetting for Eula. After all, she is not used to having strangers in her house, whereas I am used to a great deal of coming and going. So I suggested that perhaps Michaela would like to come and stay with me while she waited for you to arrive. The girl was very eager. It seems that she had seen the posters about the dance troupe and asked me about the dancers. I see now why." Mrs. Outhwaite paused. "But, really, it was as an actress I envisioned her. She has something of a gift there. If you watch, you will see — as if she could be capable of projecting a character, a personality, not necessarily her own." Mrs. Outhwaite laughed. "Of course, this is my own metier and I see her in that light. For that matter, she may already be a consummate actress able to engage your sympathies, by creating a role for herself. Has the thought not occurred to you?"

It certainly has to me, thought Julia, but she did not say this aloud.

Laura said, obviously dismayed, "I cannot really believe that Michaela has set out to deceive us. She is only a child —"

"But one perhaps who has been taught by cruel experience to take advantage through disguise."

"No, no, I won't believe that!" Laura cried. "Don't you like her?"

Mrs. Outhwaite, realizing that she had upset

Laura, said quickly, "Oh, I do, I do! She is a most obliging, considerate girl."

Downcast, Laura said, "I am sorry that I misjudged the situation. I thought that having her here for a short while would help cheer up my mother-in-law. She has been so sad since my husband died."

There was a silence after this statement. Even Mrs. Outhwaite felt the weight of Laura's words. Finally she roused herself to say, as if seeking something to lighten the atmosphere, "Would you like to see my theater? It is really a triumph of making do with what is available. I am very proud of it."

They followed her out of the room and down a corridor that led to the back of the house where there was a door that gave onto the wide graveled space. Beyond was the big red barn they had seen as they drove in, the sides of which were plastered with the remnants of placards advertising the plays that had been performed during the summer. The wide barn doors were fastened shut and a smaller door had been cut into one of them. Mrs. Outhwaite led them through this.

Inside it was dim, the great space lit only by gleams of light entering through apertures high up in the walls. As their eyes grew accustomed to the dimness they saw stacked against the walls quantities of folding chairs and at the farther end a stage. Dust motes danced in a feeble ray of light filtering down onto the stage.

Mrs. Outhwaite was saying, "We've made the hayloft into a musicians' gallery. Sometimes we have a small musical group there."

She stopped and they all three stood and gazed at the figure on the stage. Michaela, too rapt to have heard them come in, was dancing as if bewitched by her own imagination. Julia glanced at Laura. They both remembered the courtyard at the pension and Michaela's solitary dancing. Her movements now were more certain, more vigorous, as if she was emboldened by the greater space, the smooth boards under her feet.

Mrs. Outhwaite, who had stood watching, speechless, suddenly called out, "Michaela!" Her voice rang out in the vaulted quiet and the girl on the stage stopped instantly and stood motionless, as if struck.

Mrs. Outhwaite's tone of voice softened and she said, "Michaela, I had no idea you were here. I came to show these friends the theater."

Julia, intrigued by Mrs. Outhwaite's sudden change from peremptory challenge to conciliation, watched Michaela's equally swift change from a vibrant figure moving with charged energy to a docile, half-frightened girl. She stepped slowly off the stage and walked down the length of the barn towards them. As she stood quietly in front of them, with her head bowed, Laura said gently, "You do so want to dance, don't you, Michaela?"

Michaela looked up at her. Laura looked at Mrs. Outhwaite and said, "Perhaps Mrs. Outhwaite can help us."

Mrs. Outhwaite said in astonishment, "I? Well —"

Laura said firmly, "Perhaps we can talk about it."

Mrs. Outhwaite, understanding that Laura did not want to talk about it in front of Michaela, answered, "Oh, certainly, let us go back to the house."

She led them out of the barn. Michaela, Laura saw, gazed after them but stayed where she was. Mrs. Outhwaite stopped in the middle of the graveled yard and asked, "What do you want my help for?"

"To find a dancing school for Michaela," said Laura. "We know nothing about such things."

Mrs. Outhwaite did not answer at once but stood pondering. Then she said, "You must give me a little time to consider this."

On the way back to the Houghtons, Julia said, "You got Mrs. Outhwaite involved in this very easily."

"That is because she is as much intrigued by Michaela as we are."

That afternoon when Mrs. Outhwaite arrived at the Houghton house, Dilsy, ushering her in, said, "Mrs. Houghton hasn't got up from her nap yet."

"Oh, I expect I'm a little early."

"But Miss Laura is here. Shall I tell her you're here?"

"Oh, yes. I'd like to see her."

Laura, coming into the living room, found Mrs. Outhwaite seated on the sofa, lost in thought. She started when Laura greeted her and said, "This is providential. I was so anxious to talk to you that I came over earlier than I was expected."

"About Michaela?"

"Yes. I was very much struck by what we saw this morning. After you left I asked Michaela why she was doing that. I think she thought I disapproved."

"Julia and I saw her trying to dance when we were in France. That is why we decided to bring her here — to see if we could arrange for her to be taught."

"I see." Mrs. Outhwaite gazed at her for a moment. "There are schools that combine training in dance with basic education. However, children usually begin at an earlier age. But not always. Some of our greatest dancers have begun when they were older than Michaela."

Laura, realizing that Mrs. Outhwaite was still halfway talking to herself, did not reply.

Mrs. Outhwaite went on. "I have been thinking about her. She should have a chance, shouldn't she — a young thing like that. You know, I have a friend. You have heard of Lila, haven't you?"

"Lila?"

"Yes. Just Lila." Mrs. Outhwaite looked at her. "Once upon a time, when I was younger and well-known on the stage, Lila was younger, too, and known as one of the stars of our ballet theater. Now she is retired but she can't stay away from her real love, any more than I can. She teaches — she has her own ballet school. The dancers who came here at the end of summer were from her school."

Laura, afraid to distract her from her train of thought, kept silent.

Mrs. Outhwaite asked suddenly, "Shall I talk to her about Michaela?"

Laura said earnestly, "It would be a very great kindness — to Michaela and to me."

Mrs. Outhwaite considered her and presently said, "Yes, I should like to do something for you, Laura. I don't know that I should speak of this but

69

Eula has talked to me often about you and how faithful you have always been, not only to your husband, but to his parents. You know, I have never said anything to Eula in criticism of her son but I have, over the years, heard a great deal of gossip about him that did not gibe with the picture of him she gave me. I know one should not place too much credence in gossip, which is often malicious, but I've had reason to believe some of the things that have been told me by people whose opinions I respect. You have saved Eula, especially, a great deal of heartache. He was not a satisfactory husband, was he?"

Reluctantly Laura said, "I'm afraid he was weak in some ways — we all are, of course. He couldn't say No when he was being cajoled into something but afterwards he would complain bitterly that he had been misled. He even accused me of having pressed him into marrying me over his better judgment."

"So why didn't he leave you?"

"He didn't really want to. He wanted somebody to depend upon when he had doubts about himself, without admitting that this was so. He even complained that women pursued him and that he couldn't get rid of them. Yet he was very flattered by the idea that this was the case. I was a kind of protection, don't you see? If he stayed married to me, he had an escape when a situation got too hot."

"My dear, you'll forgive me when I say, how banal! But I am glad that you saw the thing to the end. I have become quite fond of Eula. She has been a warm friend to me since I moved here. She always makes me feel welcome in her house and at my age that is a valuable thing. I would not have her disillusioned for the world."

There were sounds in the hall and Dilsy appeared in the doorway with a tea trolley. Mrs. Houghton, she said, was on her way down.

Laura, escaping, fled up the stairs before she appeared. Julia was sitting in the armchair in their room, reading. She looked up in surprise. "I thought you were gone for the afternoon."

"No, thank goodness. But I've been talking to Mrs. Outhwaite, alone. She has a suggestion about Michaela." Rapidly she outlined what Mrs. Outhwaite had said."

Julia said, "As Mrs. Outhwaite would say, this is providential. Do you suppose Lila will agree to this? And I wonder how much it will cost?"

Before Laura could answer, there was a discreet knock on the door. When Julia said, "Come in," the door opened and Michaela stood on the threshold. She picked up a tray she had placed on the floor. It held two cups of tea and a plate of slices of cake. She smiled shyly and said, "Would mesdames like this here?"

When Laura smiled she put the tray down on the end table. Laura asked, "Did Mrs. Houghton tell you to bring this up?"

"Oh, no, madame Laura. I think that perhaps you would not want to come back downstairs."

As Michaela left the room, Laura and Julia exchanged glances. "How did she get here?" Julia wondered.

"She must have come with Mrs. Outhwaite," said Laura.

That evening as they had drinks in the living

room before dinner, Mrs. Houghton said, "Was Michaela here this afternoon?" When Laura said Yes she said in a vexed tone, "I told Dilsy to go and fetch you to have tea down here with Margot and me, but Dilsy said that Michaela had taken tea up to you in your room."

Aware that Mrs. Houghton was annoyed, Laura said placatingly, "I had already had a chat with Mrs. Outhwaite and I thought you would rather visit with her alone."

"Well, no," said Mrs. Houghton. "I don't like Michaela interfering that way. When she was here, before she went over to stay with Margot she wanted to wait on us at breakfast. When I asked her why she was doing that, she said she wanted to wait on us, but I explained to her that it would upset Dilsy, who is used to our looking after ourselves at breakfast time. So I told her not to do that."

Laura said, "She used to bring us tea in the afternoon when we were at the pension in France. She probably thought this was a natural thing to do."

Mrs. Houghton made no reply but Laura could see that she was still not mollified. She looked across the room at Julia, who was listening politely to a discourse by Fred Houghton on the latest political developments in Washington that affected agriculture in Virginia. Having heard the exchange between them, Julia raised an eyebrow. Later, when they were alone, she said, "Thank God for Mrs. Outhwaite — in more ways than one."

"Yes," said Laura, briefly.

* * * * *

The next day, since the weather was fine, Mrs. Houghton was persuaded to have lunch at Mrs. Outhwaite's, the draw being Orinda's cooking, which was renowned in the neighborhood. Julia drove her and Laura over. Michaela served them at the table. She has not improved at all, thought Julia, observing the clumsiness with which she passed the dishes and the mistakes she made in providing the appropriate silverware. Mrs. Outhwaite's flowing conversation carried the meal along, though Mrs. Houghton was obviously annoyed. Finally, when Mrs. Outhwaite suggested they have coffee in the living room, it was Orinda who brought in the coffee service. Laura, taking an opportunity, slipped down the hall to the kitchen.

In the big airy room Michaela sat on a stool, her arms crossed and a stubborn look on her face.

Laura said, "Michaela, you're unhappy."

But Michaela made no response. Before Laura could speak again, Orinda came back into the kitchen. She was a tall, light-skinned black woman who carried her bulk with a regal assurance. She glanced at Laura and then at Michaela but said nothing. Laura said, "I think Mrs. Outhwaite would like some more sugar for her coffee. Will you send Michaela in with it, Orinda?"

For a moment Orinda seemed about to refuse, but changed her mind and placing a sugar bowl on a small tray, handed it to Michaela without a word. Michaela got off the stool and walked out of the kitchen with the sugar bowl and without a glance at Laura or Orinda.

Laura, waiting till she was out of earshot, said, "What is the matter, Orinda? Has Michaela done something she shouldn't?"

"No, ma'am."

"I think she is very anxious to help."

Orinda made no reply.

Laura tried again. "Does she do things you don't want her to?"

"No, ma'am."

"Then what is the trouble? Is it that you don't like her?"

Orinda's large dark eyes dwelt on Laura's face for a long moment. "Well, ma'am, she's a foreigner and she does things I don't understand."

"Does she talk back to you?"

"Oh, no. She's polite. But I can't always count on her doing what I've told her to do. She almost made me spoil the souffle today and it's Mrs. Houghton's favorite. I can't always tell what she's going to do. I had to just tell her to leave things alone and stay out of my way."

"Perhaps she doesn't understand what you're saying to her."

"She certainly is ignorant about a lot of things — things you'd think anybody would know. I had to show her the difference between the refrigerator and the freezer and tell her not to put the wrong things in the wrong place. That was after she'd ruined some eggs. Wouldn't you think she would know better? I thought at first she was being smart, trying to get my goat. But I figure that's not it."

"I'm sorry she's giving you trouble. You know, she's had a very unusual sort of childhood."

The dam of Orinda's pent-up frustration was broken and her grievances spilt over. "She can be mighty clumsy. I thought maybe she was doing things on purpose because she didn't want to work here in the kitchen with me. But I think it's because she's daydreaming, not paying attention to what I'm saying. Tell you the truth, ma'am, she acts as if she's not used to living in a regular house like this, with things done in a proper way. Doesn't she have a mother? She's not been taught anything properly."

"That's entirely likely," said Laura. "In any case we're taking her back to New York in a few days. Do try to be patient with her."

"Well, ma'am, I don't mean to be harsh with her."

Michaela had not returned and Laura walked down the hall to the room that Mrs. Outhwaite referred to variously as the library or the music room. She heard Michaela's voice as she approached and a series of thumps. When she entered the room she saw that Michaela stood in the middle of the floor executing ballet steps or an attempt at them. When she saw Laura she stopped at once and stood still.

Julia, sitting in an armchair, her long legs crossed, said, "Michaela has been showing me some dance steps she has learned from studying the pictures in a book Mrs. Outhwaite has here. She says she has been practicing them in the barn."

The memory passed through Laura's mind of Michaela on the stage of the barn, a small figure dwarfed by the cavernous space, absorbed in her solitary vision. Laura felt a pang at the recollection of Orinda's complaints.

But Michaela had forgotten her own resentment. Her face was flushed from dancing and her eyes looked directly into Laura's without a trace of discomfit. She smiled. "Madame Julie was clapping for me to keep time. My first audience." Michaela bowed low to Julia, a ballet dancer's bow, with one leg stretched out behind her.

Laura said, "Michaela, we're going back to New York tomorrow. So you must get your things together."

The bright confidence in Michaela's face faded instantly. She replied obediently, "Oui, madame."

Laura, unhappy at the sight of her sudden withdrawal, hurried on. "We must find a school for you, Michaela. Mrs. Outhwaite says she may be able to help us — somewhere where you can learn to dance."

Michaela looked at her warily. It's the old Michaela, thought Laura, ready for disappointment. Michaela seemed to wait for a moment as if to see whether Laura had more to say and then went out of the room.

Laura answered Julia's glance. "I'm afraid it doesn't work, having Michaela here. She seems to disrupt things."

"So we'll be leaving tomorrow. Well, I can't say I am unhappy about that. But I must tell you: Mrs. Outhwaite, in an aside, as they say on the stage, indicated to me that she wants to talk to me privately. So you're to take Mrs. Houghton out to the car and wait for a few minutes while she does so."

Hope dawned in Laura's face. "Do you think —?"

"Maybe so. Now, don't get too hopeful."

Laura found it easier to entertain Mrs. Houghton than she had anticipated. When she went in search of her, she found her in the kitchen talking to Orinda. Orinda, she learned, was cousin to Dilsy, and Mrs. Houghton, with the instinct bred through generations, was visiting with Orinda to maintain the bridge of close relationship. Half an hour later, just as they seated themselves in the car, Julia came out of the house followed by Mrs. Outhwaite exclaiming, "So you're leaving tomorrow! But you must come back soon! We've just made acquaintance."

Laura avoided looking at Mrs. Houghton. "I'm afraid we must. Julia must get back."

Mrs. Houghton began, reproachfully, "But, dear, you did not tell me. Perhaps you can stay a little longer if Julia must leave now."

Laura, with a sense of being beleaguered, said firmly, "No, I must go back with her, to see about Michaela. We'll be back for the holidays."

In their room Laura demanded, "What did she say?"

"She has talked to Lila and according to her, Lila is willing to interview Michaela and see whether she can undertake to teach her. So, you will have to go and see Lila. I think it had better be you rather than me."

Laura sighed. Julia put her arms around her. "Cheer up, little one. It will keep you out of trouble."

＊ ＊ ＊ ＊ ＊

Julia went around opening the windows in the apartment. It was on the twelfth floor of an old building and therefore had the advantage of having a spare room and a small dining room separate from the kitchen. She had lived here for years alone except for the occasional times when Laura had stayed with her.

Laura stood next to the pile of luggage that Michaela had helped the building superintendent bring up in the elevator. Most of it had been in storage in the basement while they were in Europe and at the Houghtons. Michaela stood expectantly in the middle of the living room, watching with bright eyes as Julia moved about. Manhattan, Julia supposed, excited her with its strangeness and the sense of life it exuded.

Julia said, "Michaela, will you carry these bags into the bedroom?" She pointed in the direction she meant.

Michaela sprang into action. While she was gone Laura asked, "Where are you putting her? She slept on the sofa in here the night before we sent her to Virginia."

"That little room," said Julia. "The one I use as a study. There is a sleep-sofa in there. I'll clear my things out. We're going to have to share that desk in the corner over there. We'll all have to share the bathroom."

"What shall we do when her mother comes?"

78

"I haven't thought that far ahead. We'll have to make some sort of arrangement. It occurs to me that we won't have much privacy with Michaela here."

"Oh, I'm sure she will try not to be intrusive."

Julia's exasperation showed in her face. "Laura, the girl has eyes and ears."

"And what is she to see and hear?" Laura's voice held the haughty tone Julia sometimes heard.

"I just mean that we shall have to be careful."

"We always are," Laura rejoined. Then she relented, "Oh, darling! I know I've got us into something now. But it won't be for long."

Michaela came back into the room and stood again waiting. Julia said, "Michaela, you're going to sleep in here. Come and help me move some things out."

When she came back leaving Michaela to carry armfuls of books and papers to pile in the corner of the living room, Laura said, "It's after six. What are we going to do about a meal?"

"God!" said Julia and turned abruptly to a cabinet that stood against the wall. When she opened the door bottles of liquor were revealed. She got out glasses and a bottle. "I'll have to go down to the corner for a bag of ice. The ice trays are not filled."

"Send Michaela," said Laura.

Julia stopped in what she was doing. "Why, the kid doesn't know anything about buying a bag of ice."

"It's not an esoteric subject," Laura retorted. "She will have to learn to cope with things here."

Michaela, coming back into the room, was quick to pick up the undertone in their voices. She looked

79

from one to the other but dropped her eyes when Laura glanced at her.

Julia said carefully, "Michaela, there is a shop on the corner of this street. It sells sandwiches and soft drinks and ice cubes — glazons, vous comprendez? — in bags. The bags are in a machine and you must pay before you take a bag out. Will you please go and get us a bag?"

While she searched for money to give her, Laura added, "And get yourself anything you want to drink, Michaela."

Julia handed Michaela several bills. Michaela looked down at the money and then at her. Julia took a deep breath, and said, pointing, "This is a five dollar bill. That is a ten dollar bill. I think you will need to use the ten dollar bill, so offer that to the person in the store first. Do you understand?"

Michaela looked carefully at the bills and said with a smile, "Oh, madame Julie. I understand."

Julia added, "And remember, when you come back, you must ring the bell at our mailbox so that we can let you into the building."

Michaela smiled again. "Oh, yes, madame Julie, I know that."

Julia said under her breath as Michaela went out of the apartment door, "Her commercial instincts are in good order, at any rate."

"Well, you know, she has had to deal with several kinds of money."

"Oh, she's sharp enough. She can be a clever little spy."

"Spy?"

"On us, of course," said Julia crossly. "I know it

doesn't really matter, here, when we're alone. The people I mingle with don't really care about my private life — unless it makes for amusing gossip. None of my friends and colleagues would care if they knew or guessed we were lovers — except for the fact that I've always been alone and never have had affairs. This would have the cachet of novelty. I am not vulnerable professionally. I have tenure. But there is something else. Michaela is a minor. That might excite some interest."

Laura was silent, mulling over what Julia had said.

Then Julia asked, "Does Catharine know anything — about you and me?"

"I don't know. She was always only interested in me as Dick's wife — his inconvenient wife. I think she was always on the watch for any hint that I was having affairs of my own. But I don't know whether she ever thought of you in that light. But if she does know, what could she do about it?"

"Oh, spread the news around. And see that the Houghtons heard about it. Out of disappointment, or revenge, or just plain bitchiness."

The intercom from the downstairs door sounded. When Michaela came into the apartment carrying the bag of ice she stood for a moment till Laura, divining her dilemma, led her to the refrigerator and showed her where to place it. Orinda was right, thought Laura. There were surprising gaps in Michaela's acquaintance with the ordinary things of modern life.

* * * * *

Laura stood still on the pavement, ignoring the people hurrying past her, and looked again at the slip of paper on which she had written Lila's address. Her knowledge of Manhattan was limited to what she had seen in several brief visits over the years since she had first met Julia. Carnegie Hall was not far away, she thought. She went on down the street, searching for house numbers, till her eye fell on the large sign in the window of a converted dwelling — The New Age School of Dance.

Inside she waited for a while, seated on a chrome and plastic chair. The receptionist had invited her to sit nearby while she made telephone calls. Presently she gestured towards Laura and said, "Madame Lila will see you. Please take the elevator to the second floor."

Madame Lila, Laura mused, riding up alone in the small elevator. Evidently, like royalty, she was known only by that name. When she arrived at Lila's office, she found it to be a room crowded with files, stacked posters, oddments of various sorts, with several people standing about. Lila herself was a gaunt woman, perhaps ten years younger than Mrs. Outhwaite, with raven black hair drawn back from her face — it must be dyed, thought Laura. She was dressed in a flowing skirt and a collarless blouse that hung from her shoulders; the pale, undefined colors accentuated her bony body and deeply tanned skin. Her profile, which Laura saw first, was hawklike and her grey eyes were bold and demanding of the attention of whomever they lit upon.

With a gesture Lila cleared the room. "You're Laura Houghton?" she said. "I'm sorry I was not able to talk to you in person when you phoned. But I have a moment now. My time is so completely occupied. But since Margot sent you to me — I believe she said when she called a day or so ago — time passes very fast — something about a protegee of yours." She looked hard at Laura.

"Yes," said Laura. "A young girl. I believe Michaela may have real talent. Certainly she is very eager."

"As a dancer?"

"As a dancer. I want her to have the chance to find out if she really can learn to be a dancer."

Lila's eyes continued to dwell on Laura. "There is only one way to find out. However, many girls think they want to be dancers — have a burning ambition to be acclaimed ballerinas — and just as often it is far from the fact that they have the talent — and the fortitude to pursue the proper training."

"I realize that must be so," said Laura. "But I do want her to have a chance."

"Well, if you are prepared to find out that there is no reason to give her training —"

"I have seen her try," Laura interrupted. "Of course, she is entirely untutored. But she is so eager to learn, and she is much better coordinated when she is trying to dance than when she is engaged in other sorts of physical activity."

This statement seemed to catch Lila's attention. "That's interesting. But it might just mean that she would make a good gymnast. I am sorry to say that much of the dancing that you see nowadays is mere acrobatics. That is not the sort of dancing I teach. Mine is as pure classicism as I can make it. Only in that way can a dancer achieve the very height of her powers. If she is thoroughly disciplined in the classical mode she can do anything else afterwards that she wants. And I do not believe in creating automatons. There is more to a dancer's art than agility and physical stamina. There must be also a gift for understanding the emotions that the dance both arouses and portrays. You understand, don't you, that dance has a deep connection with sexual instinct — more so than music by itself, since it requires the use of the body. And dance is both ephemeral and everlasting. Performing a ballet is like writing in water: the moment it is over it has vanished. The choreography remains and the music but that particular projection of it has fled. Dancers can pass on to younger ones the elements of the vision they portrayed but each performance is a new occurrence — not like an artist's painting or a composer's score. That is why I say that a dancer cannot be an automaton, simply executing the intricacies of the choreography without the infusion of the dancer's own personality and spirit."

When Lila paused for breath, Laura said, "Mrs. Outhwaite said that she thinks Michaela has an actor's gift."

Lila glanced at her sharply. "Yes, Margot mentioned that to me. I pay attention to what she says about that because Margot is a great actress herself and able to recognize when someone has a natural talent for the stage. There is a connection, you know, between the achievements of the greatest ballerinas and the portrayal of character on the stage." Lila lapsed into silence for a long moment. Then she said, having apparently canvassed the situation in her own mind, "We can come to no conclusion without Michaela herself — that is her name, isn't it? — is she Portuguese? If you will bring her here, I will evaluate her. You must abide by my decision. If I think she shows promise, we can work out some scheme for training her. And for paying for that training. You understand that I do not take everyone who asks me to train them and my training is expensive. In fact, I avoid this sort of situation now. I am too old to give of myself as I used to in the past. But I cannot deny Margot when she asks this of me."

That evening, Julia said, after hearing Laura's account of her interview with Lila, "It's amazing that she agreed. I've heard something about Lila in the last few days."

"She said it would be expensive," Laura reminded her.

"Well, I suppose between us we can manage."

Laura, sitting slumped in a large armchair, said, "I suppose it depends on what impression Michaela makes on her. I worry about that. Sometimes she seems to put people off."

"You feel that way because of Mrs. Houghton, who does not like any disruption of the even tenor of her life. Don't let her discourage you, darling. Michaela must make her own way."

"It is simply that she is so naive — yes, naive. I know you suspect her of being devious, but I don't think that is so. She is so accepting of everyone and everything. She does not question what people do or say. She doesn't look for a meaning below the surface. She acts as if she believes she must accept what is said or done to her, because she has no right to complain or protest. I think that is very sad."

"Well, if that is the case, it means that she has so little information about the world, she can't make a comparison of people or what they say. Oh, I know she has had a hard life for a fourteen-year-old. But that mother of hers does not seem to have given her any standards to judge things by. One thing — one person — is as good — or bad — as another. So she doesn't question what she is told or what she sees happen; she doesn't look for an explanation." Julia paused. "Either that, or she is stupid. And we know she is not stupid. She has her own ideas about things and people but she knows by instinct that she shouldn't voice them. Yes, I suppose that is a sad state of affairs in the case of such a young girl. All right, Laura dear, I shan't think of her as devious." Perhaps, Julia thought privately, I just don't want the emotional burden of being responsible for her happiness.

The next day, all through her usual activities, the thought of Michaela came into Julia's mind: how was she doing in the interview with Lila? She found herself trying to imagine what Michaela's response would be when Laura presented her to Lila. Lila, Laura said, was a formidable woman, large featured with a peremptory manner that was doubtless exaggerated by age. Would Michaela be frightened and withdraw into herself in that maddening, mute unresponsiveness, that wooden passivity that was so frustrating to anyone who sought to draw her out? Julia was relieved when, at noon, Laura called to say that Michaela had passed the first test. Lila had agreed to give her an audition. She was to go for it the next day.

"How is Michaela?"

"She's very quiet. I expect she is frightened."

"Did Lila scare her?"

"To some extent, I suppose. But I think she is more frightened at the idea of what this will mean if Lila takes her as a pupil. Because, you see, she has never had a glimmer of a chance before this to do something that means more to her than anything else in the world. Wouldn't you be?"

"The great unknown. Yes, I see what you mean. She knows what it is to be frightened of unknown places, unknown people, threatening events. But joy ?"

"Yes," said Laura. "Sometimes it is hard to believe that the future holds something good, something wonderful."

The following evening when Julia opened the door of the apartment and stepped inside she was aware of the stillness as if the place was empty — the feeling so familiar to her of returning to an empty home. Laura, then, must still be out. But Laura was there, sitting at the desk in the corner of the room. She looked up and glanced at Julia absentmindedly.

Impatient, Julia said, "Well, what happened?"

"I'm not sure."

"You're not sure?"

"I mean, Lila had Michaela do some exercises on the barre — working at the barre, I think they call it — you know, standing by a bar fixed along the wall and lifting her legs in certain patterns, which Lila demonstrated to her. She's all on wires — Lila — you know, and her muscles are as hard as if she was twenty years younger. At first she was very talkative, as she was the first time I saw her and then she began to slow down until finally she was silent. Then presently she told Michaela that that was enough. Of course Michaela was very stiff and awkward and when Lila told her to stop she just froze in place, as if that was the end for her. But Lila did something surprising. She went over to her and began to manipulate her arms and legs. Like this, she said, you must move like this, and you must relax your muscles. Michaela just stood there, looking at the floor. Lila looked at her for a few minutes and then patted her and said, 'It's all right, little one. We must see what we can do.' "

"What did Michaela do?"

"She plodded away to where her clothes were and began to put them on. Any other girl would have burst into tears. Do you suppose Michaela has any tears — or have they all been bred out of her? My heart ached for her. I wanted to try to reassure her, but I could not just then. I had no idea what Lila meant to do."

"Did you find out?"

Laura hesitated. "When she left Michaela, she turned to me and said that she had no more time just then, but she wanted to talk to me further, without Michaela being present. I am to go and see her tomorrow morning. Could you possibly come with me?"

Julia made a rapid calculation of her professional schedule. "I think I can, if it doesn't take too long."

"I'm afraid that what she wants to propose is vital and I'd like to have your support."

"And where is Michaela now?"

Laura turned her head as if listening for sounds from elsewhere in the apartment. "She's in her room. On the way home she was — or seemed to be — what she was when we first met her — very remote."

"That is probably her way of absorbing disappointment."

"But you know I feel there is no cause for her to be disappointed. I think Lila intends to take her on. But I don't know and I can't raise false hopes." Laura looked up at Julia in anguish.

"Oh, darling! Why do you get yourself so involved in these things! You've had enough anguish of your own. I thought we were leaving all that behind us."

Laura leaned her head against Julia. "I am so on edge. You know, Michaela could simply run away, in despair, just disappear. Then what should we do?"

Julia, shocked at the idea, tried to sweep it away. "Michaela? No, she would not do that. I'm sure she wouldn't." But Julia was inwardly not so certain. She decided to change the subject. "What shall we do with her while we're talking to Lila?"

"Why, she can amuse herself as she did today. I think she spent the day visiting Macy's. I know she went on the bus. She seems to be afraid of the subway. She says it is not like the Metro in Paris. I gave her some pocket money and I told her about the Metropolitan Museum."

"Museums don't seem quite to be Michaela's style — unless there is some sort of exhibit concerning ballet," said Julia.

"Well, I think I had better go and find her and

see what we can arrange for dinner tonight. She is
no cook but she'll do what I tell her. Perhaps I can
cheer her up."

They arranged to meet the next morning at Lila's
school. Laura stood on the sidewalk waiting when
Julia arrived. When they entered Lila's office it was
empty. In the distance they could hear the sharp
cries of a dance instructor in a nearby room and the
floor of the old building trembled slightly under the
thumps of the dancers' feet. Presently Lila appeared,
moving quickly across to sit behind her desk. She
nodded and gave Julia a sharp, evaluating look as
Laura spoke her name. Julia, Laura explained, had
equal responsibility for Michaela.

Lila nodded, as if this was a foregone conclusion.
Then, speaking almost disdainfully, as if she was not
used to accounting to anyone for her decisions, she
said, "I wanted to speak to you before I made any
announcement about my impression of Michaela. To
begin with, Margot was quite right. The girl has
unusual potential. But as what? That we must
discover. I think she will be a dancer. There is
something in her, in the way she moves, the fire
that burns beneath the surface. And I do not think
she will be capricious — enthusiastic now and losing
interest tomorrow. No, that is not this girl. She is
strong and vigorous. She must come from hardy
people, who know how to survive misfortune."

As she paused, Laura broke in. "Then you will
undertake to teach her?"

Lila held up a large, bony hand to stop her. "Not
so fast. There is another matter that must be
resolved first. It is the question of the cost. You are

not wealthy women." She looked boldly at Laura and then Julia.

"No," said Julia. "But anything within reason —"

"Ah, yes," Lila cut her short. "But you must understand. There is wonderful raw material here. I have seldom seen anything to compare with it in my years of teaching. She can be trained, she can learn the routines, she can master the techniques. She has energy, she has the desire to excel. But classical dance is not something that will be achieved in a day, a week, a year. She must dedicate herself to this, so that as she grows in knowledge, in experience, in understanding, she can develop her gift."

"She is only fourteen," said Laura meekly.

"Ah, yes." Lila sat back in her chair. "A little old for a start in such a career. But too young to have depth, to show beyond a doubt that she has the qualities that will make it possible for her to achieve what appears to be her potential. Fame, fortune, acclaim — all may be possible, but how can one say that she will in fact achieve all this at the end of the long journey, through years of devoted teaching, endless effort?"

Lila suddenly jumped up from her chair and paced around the room. "How can we know? I hold back, I try not to allow one more enthusiasm to take charge of me. I know the cost to me. I have learned it over the years. Michaela must be ready to spend years of sacrifice, of enormous physical and mental effort. But I will have to, too. And I am an old woman." She suddenly, as suddenly as she had leapt up, broke off her outburst. "She will come here and

I will teach her what she must know. The rest is up to her. How can we know what is in her mind? What does she really seek?"

Laura thought, how can you see into Michaela? There are her eyes that can be so black, so impenetrable, so shutting out of your gaze except for moments when something flashes, which leave you uncertain about your judgment of her. Obviously Lila felt this uncertainty, this ambiguity.

Julia spoke, "This means that you are going to undertake to teach her."

Lila stopped in front of Julia, as if all at once aware that she was there. "Yes. I don't deny that, as a teacher, I feel the attraction of taking an untutored girl and setting her feet on the road — the long, long road — to the goal of all great dancers: to be a prima ballerina — the greatest of prima ballerinas. I see much reason to hope. She moves to music as if it is her natural element. She is absorbed in what she is doing. She is not trying to show off, to try to please. She dances as if she is compelled to dance. Her body is called into motion by some instinct, something compelling beyond her own will. Yes, I find there is enormous attraction in the idea of teaching Michaela."

Again she paused and looked from one to the other of them. "And now, since you understand what we are undertaking, we must speak of money. You see what expense will be involved — time and expense. There are risks involved here too — accidents, changes in the girl herself. I must demand compensation for my time and the risks I take. Are you prepared for that?"

Julia said with a note of caution in her voice,

"We must have some estimate of what it will take — by the year, at least. And you realize, we have no legal authority over Michaela. She is a minor and her mother may not agree to your program for her. We cannot speak for her."

Lila had sat down again at her desk and had picked up a pencil, the end of which she was gnawing. Her brilliant grey eyes roved from one to the other of them. "There is something I can suggest. Do you think we can plan on a year? If her mother sees the progress she makes in a year, perhaps all doubt will be removed about the importance of this to her daughter's future."

Laura interrupted. "I have told you, Lila, that we met Michaela abroad, that her mother is still in France, and that we are not certain that she will approve of a career in dance for her."

"Yes, but how stupid of her not to realize that this is the chance of a lifetime for Michaela! If I begin teaching her, I do not intend to be thwarted if I see the promise developing that I suspect. But we can postpone that for a short while."

"What is your suggestion?" Julia asked.

Lila looked at her out of eyes that were now shrewd. "I have a friend who likes little girls. No, it's not a man. I see the suspicion in your eyes. No, Miriam Rudolph is also quite insane about ballet. I believe that when she was very young she had a great desire to be a dancer herself, but her family — very wealthy, conservative people — would have none of it. So now that she is widowed and her own mistress she likes to support girls who need financial assistance to become dancers. She has provided many scholarships for girls who study with me; she trusts my judgment in picking out the girls. But I've never had the opportunity to offer her such a choice as Michaela. I don't think that there is any doubt that Mrs. Rudolph will be ready to help."

"But," said Julia, "there is the uncertainty about Michaela's mother. She is still in France. When she consented to allow Michaela to come with us, we had no definite plan, do you see? Her mother was just eager for Michaela to come here to the States in search of opportunity. I don't think you should approach Mrs. Rudolph until we are more certain about her attitude."

Lila plainly did not like this temporizing. She said, with an arrogant note, "In the ordinary way I would not consider doing what I have suggested — teach a girl who has no background of any sort. If I have decided to undertake this, I intend to go on with it. The girl is here, under your care. You will be responsible for her expenses till her mother comes and we can settle that question then."

* * * * *

They stood on the sidewalk, silent, for some minutes. Then Julia said, "I find this a very unsatisfactory state of affairs."

Laura, who had been waiting for her to speak, answered, "We don't seem to have a choice. We can't tell Michaela that she can't go to Lila, if Lila says she wants her."

"But suppose she does go on and is well underway when her mother arrives and her mother says, No, she can't go on."

"Do you think she would?"

"I've no idea. But if she does, there's nothing we can do about it."

"But, Julie, dear, we can't let Michaela miss this chance — even if it comes to nothing. And I think Lila has a point: if she makes good progress, why should her mother object? It is a way for them both to live."

"And what about us?" Julia demanded.

"It's only for a little while. You know that I promised Mother Houghton that we would be down again at the Christmas holidays. That gives Michaela time to show what she is capable of."

"Well, I've got to get back to work. I can't kiss you here." Julia looked at Laura and Laura smiled.

When Laura reached the apartment and put her key in the door, the sound obviously alerted Michaela. As she came into the hall, the girl was standing in the doorway of the living room. Poor child, thought Laura; she has been holding her breath all morning. Michaela seemed to take fright and disappeared toward the kitchen. Laura called, "Michaela."

Michaela came back into the room slowly. Laura, watching her, saw the tenseness in her face and body, as if she was ready once more to run away from bad news.

Laura put her hands on Michaela's arms, which hung rigid at her sides. They were almost of a height and she looked into Michaela's eyes, which were blank, hiding the misery behind them.

"Michaela," Laura said, "Madame Lila has decided to teach you to dance. You are to begin right away.

We must buy you the proper clothes. She has told me what to get."

Michaela did not stir.

Laura said anxiously, "You understand what I am saying, don't you? We'll go tomorrow to get your things." She felt a strong tremor go through Michaela's body. She put her arms around her and drew her close. "Poor child. You have been so anxious, haven't you? But I could not say anything to you before this because it was not certain." Laura hugged her a little closer, eager to dispel the rigidity in Michaela's body. Suddenly Michaela relaxed against her. Laura waited for the tears, but none came. Slowly Michaela drew away from her. Her face was flushed and she still looked at the floor.

Her voice was very low when she said, "Oui, madame Laure. I understand."

Probably, thought Laura, moving away, she isn't used to being hugged or kissed. Her mother does not seem to be a demonstrative woman. Laura said, "Come and sit down here, Michaela. I must say something else to you."

Laura walked over to the sofa and sat down, pointing to the seat beside her. Michaela obeyed, sitting stiffly.

Laura said, "Michaela, your mother does not know about this arrangement yet. Have you told her about Lila?"

"No, madame."

"Then I must write to her and tell her about this opportunity for you. Do you think she will be pleased?"

There was a long silence before Michaela answered. "I do not know, madame. Maman does not understand about dancing. She does not think it is respectable."

"I see. I shall have to explain the situation to her."

Michaela nodded and after a moment, while Laura still looked at her in perplexity, she got up and walked back to the kitchen.

When Julia arrived home that evening and Laura told her about Michaela's reception of her news, Julia said, "That sounds like Michaela. She's overwhelmed. I don't think she is used to good fortune."

"Do you suppose she took it in? And what about her mother? She does not think that her mother will approve of her learning to dance."

They looked at each other for a long moment. Then Julia said, "Well, we'll just have to go day by day. We don't have a program for what we are doing."

Laura put her head on Julia's shoulder. "I suppose this is not a sensible thing we are doing, but I feel there is a great fire in Michaela that has always been tamped down. That would be a difficult thing for an adult to deal with. It is terrible to see a young girl so fearful of expressing her feelings, especially when they are so strong."

"Perhaps dancing will be the way she will outgrow that."

* * * * *

Laura and Julia usually ate their breakfast in the kitchen, before finishing dressing for the day. Michaela, quick to divine their habits, laid plates and cutlery on the small table, anticipating their appearance. The tea that Laura drank was already brewed. This was something she knew how to do. For Julia she set out a cup and the coffee maker. She had never seen one like this before. She watched attentively while Julia made the coffee, but she made no attempt to imitate her. While they ate, she stood nearby, leaning against a kitchen cabinet, shaking her head when one of them suggested that she sit down with them. Julia supposed that she had already eaten whatever it was she ate for breakfast; Laura provided croissants and brioche, on the supposition that these suited Michaela's French habits.

This morning, Laura, after a wakeful night, during which she had worried over Michaela's response to Lila's offer, came into the kitchen early. At first she thought the room, dimly lit only by the first daylight, was empty, but when she flipped the switch and the light flooded the room, she saw Michaela sitting on a high stool with her head bowed on her folded arms.

"Why, Michaela, good morning! Whatever is the matter?"

Michaela's head had jerked up at the sudden flood of light. Her first gaze at Laura was somber. Almost at once the brief image of tragedy vanished and she was her usual impassive self.

"Nothing, madame Laure. I did not know it was so late." She jumped down from the stool and hurriedly began to collect the things to put on the table.

Laura said anxiously, "You remember, don't you, that you're to come with me this morning to get your dancing things?"

"Oui, madame."

Defeated by the automatic response, Laura went back to the bedroom. Julia, coming out of the shower, looked at her in surprise. "What's the matter?" she asked, throwing her towel over a chair.

Laura, her eyes dwelling absently on Julia's firm fifty-year-old body and long legs, said, "I think Michaela is pretty upset. I should have thought that by now she would have taken in what I told her and that she would be happy."

Julia drew on a pair of panties. Laura continued to watch her, desire lurking under her preoccupation. Julia said, "Do you suppose she has had another letter from her mother? You know, the mail is delivered here in the afternoon. She always puts yours and mine on my desk. She could have had a letter from her mother with news that has upset her. Do you suppose her mother has changed her mind about coming here and has told her she has to go back?"

"She can't do that! I can't imagine that she would have the money for plane fare for Michaela."

"Unless she uses the money you gave her for her own fare here."

"But that's impossible!" Laura, who had moved closer to Julia, turned away. "If she is not coming, she should return the money. That would be dishonest."

"Some people are," said Julia sardonically. "And

how would you make her return it, if she decides not to come? I think you had better ask Michaela some questions."

But Laura, postponing any interrogation until they had finished breakfast and Julia had left the apartment, found it was unnecessary. Coming back from the front door where she had kissed Julia goodbye she saw Michaela standing in the doorway to the kitchen as if waiting for her.

As usual, Michaela waited for her to initiate the conversation. So Laura, recognizing this, said, "Well, Michaela."

Michaela said, "Madame Laure, I have received a letter from my maman. She says that she is also writing to you to tell you about — les negoces — what do you say — the question about the lease."

"Is she having trouble?"

Michaela shook her head. "She says that it is taking longer than she expected. Mme. Guerin is helping her. But she is not receiving any money —"

"She has no income."

"No, madame, and she is worried about what she will do."

"Does she need money now?"

"Not now. But if she has to wait too long, she will use up what she has. That is why she wants me to earn some money here, now, so that we will have some when she gets here."

"How does she expect you to do that?"

"She said that you could find some work for me but I was to be careful about the sort of place and the kind of people who might want to hire me."

"You will not be earning any money while you are learning with Lila, but you do have a safe place to live and of course we'll look after you in every other way."

Michaela raised her head and looked at her in despair. "But, madame Laure, don't you see? Maman will not want me to do anything that I do not earn money for. She will forbid me."

"Forbid you to accept Lila's offer?" Laura's indignation burst out. "Michaela, we cannot allow that! She must understand what a chance this is for you."

Mutely Michaela gazed back at her. Laura reached out to touch her, and said more gently, "I shall write to her. I am sure she will not stop you. So she does not know when she will be coming."

"No, madame. She says she is explaining all this in the letter she is sending you. Perhaps it will come today."

"Yes," said Laura, getting up. "And in the meanwhile, we must go out and get you your dancing clothes. Aren't you looking forward to this, Michaela — looking forward to having real dancing shoes — though I expect you are a little frightened, too, aren't you?"

All at once Michaela's eyes flashed a brilliant ray of eagerness that vanished at once. She began to walk to her room. "I will get ready, madame."

* * * * *

With Michaela going off to dancing class every day, a routine was established for all three of them. Laura, whose income depended on what she wrote for publication and who could therefore work anywhere, set up her typewriter and papers at

Julia's desk in the corner of the living room. The desk was not meant for the use to which she put it, since it was a graceful, fragile antique that Julia had at some time acquired because she liked it. Ordinarily, when Julia worked at home, she used the little room in which Michaela now slept. The file cabinet and her reference books had been pushed into a corner to make room for Michaela, whose sparse belongings were stowed in a small space cleared in the closet where more of Julia's things were stored.

Michaela still laid the table in the kitchen for their breakfast and waited until they had finished before she got ready to leave. Laura was aware that she must be arriving at Lila's dance studio well before Lila's staff was ready for the day's work. Laura hoped that Lila was not annoyed by this. But when she inquired, Lila, surprisingly, said, "Oh, no. She is not a bother. She tidies things up around here, before the others arrive, and if she has time she goes into the studio and practices at the barre — with no music, with no one to keep count. And then, later, she makes herself useful looking after the little ones, who always need help getting their things on. My big girls don't mind her at all."

Laura, out of curiosity, went one morning to watch the class. "Come, come," Lila had ordered her. "You can see what is happening." Michaela, a big girl among a lot of little ones, stood patiently at one side as the teacher admonished those who failed to heed instructions. Michaela watched the teacher intently. When Laura had first stood in the doorway, Michaela had seen her and waved her hand. But after that she seemed to forget Laura's presence and anything else extraneous to the class activities.

Michaela came home early in the afternoon, carrying school books, and dutifully shut herself into her room to do homework. Lila had said that she would not be able to continue with her dancing lessons unless she completed each day's school work. Laura wondered how she was managing with a strange curriculum in a language she knew chiefly as a spoken tongue. Laura made a point of being visible and unoccupied when Michaela let herself into the apartment, tacitly offering help if Michaela wanted it. But Michaela simply greeted her politely and went on into her room. When Laura inquired of Lila, Lila said casually, "Oh, she does very well. She is used to studying. They taught her that in the French school."

It was Julia who insisted that Michaela eat with them in the evening. "We can't have her eating by herself in the kitchen. That isn't civilized." Laura was relieved, because it was Julia who suffered more from Michaela's intrusion into their private lives. When they did not go out to eat — and they seldom did during this period of their lives — Laura prepared dinner. She was startled the first time Michaela appeared in the kitchen while she was peeling potatoes and gently took the knife out of her hand to finish the job. It was true that Michaela was clumsy and surprisingly ignorant about the preparation of food. But she accepted correction without sullenness or resentment. It was as if, Laura told Julia, she realized her own lack of skill and expected to be corrected.

103

Julia, in bed at night, when Laura talked of this, said, "Probably she is used to being corrected much more harshly than you correct her."

"Well, I think she exasperated Orinda, who was nervous about her anyway."

"I was thinking of her mother. She had no patience with Michaela at all. She acted as if the girl was stupid — so that we thought so, too, in the beginning. Or maybe that's not quite right. You were captivated by her from the beginning."

Laura, curled up beside her, gave a little laugh. "Don't tell me that you're jealous of Michaela." When Julia reached under her to bring her into a close embrace, she went on, "I don't know just why this should be, but ever since Michaela has been here in the apartment I've been thinking more and more about you — about how you look when you're naked, about your body and how it feels when I touch you, how I feel when you touch me. Her being here with us seems to arouse something. I've been very trying, haven't I, Julie dear, for the last — what, year?"

Julia, moving her lips along Laura's jaw, murmured, "Fighting off fear and despair isn't the best atmosphere for love-making — unless you just want sex to forget your troubles."

At the dinner table Michaela sat silent. Her table manners, Laura noticed, were tidy but unsophisticated, as if she had always been used to eating in the kitchen. Glancing at her Laura saw that her plate was always empty almost before they had started to eat. As she hastened to serve her another helping she thought, after all, she is active all day long and she is a healthy, strong girl. Perhaps she has not always had enough to eat. Michaela seemed to watch them from under her eyebrows and as time went on, seemed to make some effort to imitate them.

Julia was determined that Michaela should take part in the dinner table conversation. She asked, "Well, Michaela, have you made some friends at the school? There are some girls your age, aren't there?"

Michaela stopped eating and answered slowly without looking at Julia. "There are some big girls — jeunes filles —" She glanced at Laura as if checking to see whether Laura understood what she meant. "They come for the evening and sometimes they arrive early, before I leave. They have jobs." She paused. "Some of them work as models. They are very closed — they know each other well because they have been together for some time, with Madame Lila." She looked at Laura again as if seeking help in explaining what she meant.

Laura said, "You mean, they are a clique. They do not welcome you into their group."

"Oui, madame, c'est vrai."

Julia asked, "Are they all girls from around here?"

"I do not know. I think some of them are not Americans, but they come later, after I have left. And they don't want to talk to me. They are finishing their training. They don't talk to anyone except Madame Lila."

"And how about those women who work for Lila? Aren't they friendly?"

"They are kind but they don't speak much to me. They think I will be there only a little while and it is not important to know me."

Julia looked at Laura. She said, "That sums up the situation pretty well, doesn't it?"

Laura did not answer. Michaela, noticing that they had finished their meal, got up as she did every evening and began to clear the table. Laura followed her into the kitchen to supervise. Michaela seemed to take it for granted that Laura should sit at the kitchen table and direct her what to do. I'm sure, thought Laura, this is what her mother does. And she sees no reason to burden herself with the effort of learning to act on her own. Probably she thinks whatever she does, it will be wrong.

Laura went back into the living room, saying, under her breath, "Poor child."

Julia looked up from what she was reading. "Poor child?"

"I don't believe she will ever learn that there is a system to loading the dishwasher or a proper way to choose the containers for leftovers. I think she just shuts her mind and does as she is told."

"Maybe it is a reflex action, to keep away from learning to do something she does not want to do. She may not be doing it intentionally — it is just a sort of passive resistance."

"And another thing. She takes nothing for granted. I've realized that she must be hungry when she comes home from school and it is a long time to dinner. So I have left a brioche out on the kitchen table and I've told her she can have some milk or a soft drink with it if she wants. But she doesn't touch it without coming to ask me if she may have it. I've said, yes, it is there for her; she need not ask me every time. But the next time it is the same thing over again."

"Do you remember that Madame Guerin said she could not be a gypsy because she was honest? She's probably afraid to take anything for granted."

Laura exclaimed, "Oh, darling! Even if she were a gypsy, we should not assume that she must be a thief!"

"Now, now. I'm not speaking for myself nor for you. But you have the evidence of Mme. Guerin, that old prejudices die hard." Julia paused and then asked, "What is her room like?"

"Absolutely neat and clean. She could pack up her few little things and walk out and you'd never know anyone had been there."

"That's another traditional habit of the gypsies — stealing away in the night. Perhaps she has enough inheritance from her mother to modify these instincts."

"Julia! You offend me."

"Why? All I'm saying is, that if you're a vagabond, you haven't much chance to develop regular habits."

"She's not a vagabond."

Well, I must admit, her mother doesn't strike me as being a true vagabond. But their lives have been pretty itinerant. Can you be a respectable vagabond?"

"Oh, Julia!"

"I tell you what, darling. You feel hurt because she is withholding her trust from you, in spite of all you do for her. Do remember that there is a great deal in her short life that we know nothing about."

When she had finished in the kitchen, Michaela came to the door and stood for a moment, waiting for them to notice her. Julia, looking up, said, "Come and sit down, Michaela. Is there something you'd like to do?"

Michaela obediently came and sat down on a straight chair. She did not answer Julia's question. "Do you like to go to the movies? However, I don't think you ought to go out alone after dark like this — until you are more used to this neighborhood."

Michaela said, "Yes, madame Julie."

"Is there something you like to look at on TV?" asked Laura. "You know how to find programs on that little set in your room, don't you?"

Michaela nodded.

"Well, then, would you like to go to your room?"

As if relieved, Michaela got up and saying Goodnight, mesdames, left them quickly as if eager to escape.

For a few minutes Julia and Laura sat silent. Then Laura said, "You know, I've heard music turned down very low, as if she had the radio on. Do you suppose she practices before she goes to bed?"

"In that little room?"

"Faux de mieux," said Laura.

"In that case, we should get her some cassettes of ballet music."

Julia not only bought the cassettes; she also brought home books about ballet — instruction books, appreciation books, autobiographies — which she diligently set herself to read. How like Julia, thought Laura: nothing that caught her interest could go unexplained, unstudied. Julia said nothing about

what she was reading, either to Laura or to
Michaela, but she seemed to focus her attention
more often and more fixedly on Michaela, as if
testing her new knowledge by observation.
Occasionally, she used a technical term or made a
reference to some well-known dancer. She also took
to reading reviews by dance critics in the *New York
Times* and these she sometimes read aloud to Laura.

* * * * *

One morning as she was leaving for the dance
studio, Michaela lingered for a moment close to
where Laura sat, as if she had something to say.
Laura, about to settle down to work at Julia's desk,
looked up and said, "What is it, Michaela?"

"Madame Laure, madame Lila is going to have a
recital for the little ones so that their mothers can
come and see how they are learning."

"A recital? Only for the little ones? You are not
included?" Embarrassed at the idea of tall, sturdy
Michaela in a recital with little girls half her age,
Laura stopped.

But Michaela was unconcerned. "No, madame Lila
has been teaching me by myself. She is going to
have me dance a solo."

Gazing at her, Laura suddenly realized what
Michaela was leaving unsaid: there would be no
audience for herself. Impulsively she said, "Michaela,
do you want me to come — for you?"

"Oh, yes!" There was unusual eagerness in
Michaela's voice. "Perhaps you and madame Julie
would like to come and see if I am doing well."

"Has madame Lila suggested this?"

109

Michaela hesitated. "She has not said so, but I think she would like it, too. She knows that madame Julie has given me some cassettes to study and that I am learning more about the proper music."

Bless Julia! thought Laura. "Of course, Michaela, I will come. But I doubt if Julia will be able to. When is this to take place?"

"Next Monday, in the afternoon."

"Then please tell Lila that I will come — that I want to see the progress you have made."

A brief, brilliant smile lit Michaela's face before she turned and ran out of the apartment.

Michaela did not mention the recital again, even when she left for the dance studio on Monday morning. At two in the afternoon, when Laura arrived there, she wondered if she was indeed expected, for she had heard nothing from Lila. However, no one in the studio outer office showed surprise when she came in. Perhaps, thought Laura, they don't really pay much attention to anyone who comes and goes in this throng. The studio was a little world of its own, removed from the world outside except for the wider sphere of dance beyond the school. The women of the staff at first did not give her a second glance; they were used to well-dressed matrons who spoke with foreign accents. But then the fact that she was neither a dancer nor the mother of a pupil seemed to catch their eye. One of the women got up and said, "Are you here for the recital?" and when Laura said Yes, led her down a corridor to a room where she could sit among the mothers of the little girls, on chairs ranged in a row from which the whole studio could be viewed. The little girls filled the floor of the studio, posturing and pirouetting, excited by the attention focused on them. Then their program ended and they and their mothers erupted into a hubbub of sound and motion. After a few minutes they had all gone into an adjoining room where refreshments were laid out on a table.

Laura sat still. Presently she saw Michaela come through a door at the other end of the room. She was alone. But then another dancer, an older student, came and stood by the piano. Lila suddenly reappeared and made a peremptory gesture and the girl sat down at the piano, watching Lila over her shoulder. Michaela, Laura saw, had straightened up when she saw Lila and with a light spring placed her feet in the first position, her heels together at an angle. Lila called out, "At the barre!" and obediently Michaela sprang across to the bar fixed to the wall, and as Lila counted she went quickly, with a light spring each time, through the steps that Laura recognized as the four basic positions of a dancer's feet in ballet. When she finished she came to a stop and waited, still with her eyes fixed on the floor until Lila called out, "Very good. Now —" Lila continued to issue orders, which Michaela obeyed instantly and energetically. Finally Lila said, "Now, let us go through the first passage of Spring Zephyr, which we have been practicing." She gestured to the girl at the piano, who began to play a Chopin etude.

Michaela, as if she had been freed from a leash, bounded into a series of leaps and little runs, ending in a pirouette. Laura watched in astonishment. The stolid earthbound girl she had hitherto seen suddenly was transformed into a creature of air and grace, no longer heavy-footed. The expression on her face was that of someone transfixed by a vision unseen by those beholding her. When she came to a stop, she stood for a moment in the final position, rigid, still filled with the emotion that had held her in its grip through the dance. Laura gazed at her, entranced by the clean lines of the young body, the vibrant muscles of the legs and thighs, the hollowed stomach, the firm breasts just beginning to swell. When Lila said, at Laura's elbow, "It's amazing, is it not? Clumsy, of course, scarcely any real discipline yet. But there is fire there, a sense of what is to be achieved. I see her as Giselle, as Juliet. Once she has the schooling, the discipline, she will be able to release the dancer that dwells within her."

Laura murmured, "It is a transformation. She is not a little girl any longer."

Lila looked down at her with amusement in her eyes. "Ha! She has lost all that puppy fat, hasn't she? You see the woman she will be." Lila contemplated Michaela, who now stood passive, no longer vibrant, her head hanging forward a little in the stance Laura found so pathetic and familiar. But Lila continued to talk about her, as if she could not hear, or as if it did not matter that she did. In fact, Lila seemed to be talking more to herself than to Laura, who was largely at sea in the flood of ballet terms and choreographic references. Then Lila clapped her hands and once more Michaela sprang to life, responding to the pianist's music. This time, while she danced Lila called out instructions and admonishing comments, with side remarks to Laura.

"Of course, she has had no opportunity to dance with others, to learn the proper way to respond to the movements of a group. That must be the next thing I must teach her."

Lila walked away across the room to Michaela, to take hold of her arms and position her legs and feet, making caustic comments all the while. Michaela did not seem to resent anything she did or said but was pliant and eager to achieve what Lila required.

"I had no idea that girl had got so thin."

Laura, startled by Julia's voice, looked up to see her standing beside her chair, where Lila had been. "I didn't expect you."

"I didn't say I would come because I didn't know whether I could."

"How much did you see?"

"Just the end of the dance. But she is surprising. It lifts your heart up, doesn't it, to see her spring like that, as if the floor was just a launch pad for flight through the air."

Laura looked up at her, gratified. She had seldom heard this uninhibited, glowing tone in Julia's voice. Julia's eyes were fixed on Michaela, as if she was drinking in every curve and motion of her body.

Lila's voice intruded. She had come back across the room. "Now, you see, she has a dancer's body — all sinew and strength and yet she has those fine breasts, so firm and young. I do not approve of this fad of starving girls till they are like sticks."

Laura, turning her head to look at Lila, saw the same enraptured gaze on her face as on Julia's. She said, "So there is no question now that she is yours — you will teach her?"

"Oh, none at all! None at all!" Lila exclaimed.

* * * * *

Back in the routine of days in the apartment,
Michaela showed no sign that the triumph of the
recital had changed her. She was as subdued and
submissive as before — hugging it all to herself,
thought Laura, as she has always done. But perhaps
there had been a change. Underneath her passivity
there seemed now to be a greater self-assurance that
manifested itself in an even greater patience in
listening to what was said to her. Before, Laura had
sometimes thought, she shut out the words spoken
in admonition and advice. Now she seemed to listen
more carefully, though she still showed no response
except acquiescence. Was this an effect that Lila had
had? Laura found herself seeking moments when she
could catch an unguarded glimpse of Michaela — a
furtive sort of visual eavesdropping. One such
moment came one afternoon when Michaela had
returned from the dance studio and, after letting
herself into the apartment, had tiptoed past Laura
in an effort not to disturb her as she sat writing.
Laura did not speak, had not broken off her work as
she often did, eager now to get down on paper the
thought she was pursuing, only vaguely aware of
Michaela's arrival.

Presently Laura looked up, suddenly conscious
that Michaela was in the apartment. She had a view
down the short hallway to the bedrooms. She
watched as Michaela postured in front of the
full-length looking glass on the bathroom door. She
wore her practice clothes — a long tee-shirt and a
pair of tights that reached to her ankles. She raised
her arms over her head, brought them down in a

sweeping gesture as she bent at the waist to one side and then to the other. Then she brought her hands down each side of her body, caressing it with a prideful, loving gesture. Laura could see from the expression on her face that she was enthralled, carried away into some daydream that insulated her from the world. Laura remembered the glimpses of her in the courtyard in France, in Mrs. Outhwaite's barn. But this was no longer the child exulting in the freedom of her body, away from curious eyes. This was a girl teetering on the brink of womanhood, aware of a burgeoning vitality, of a promise of the strength and grace dwelling in her body.

Laura made a slight sound to end her own voyeurism. Michaela dropped her arms instantly and resumed the quiet watchfulness that was her usual manner.

"How did you do today, Michaela?"

"We were very busy, madame. Madame Lila has several new pupils."

"Little ones?"

"Not all of them. There are some girls who want to audition for a chance to dance in the new ballets that are being staged this season. There are companies coming from abroad and they need to hire dancers for their corps de ballet."

"Is there any chance that you could qualify?"

Michaela's eyes suddenly widened. "Oh, no! I am not ready yet. Madame Lila would not permit me. I have so much to learn. She says she does not want me to get bad habits by dancing with others till she thinks I am ready. But it is very interesting to see what these girls do. They have been trained in other schools — not like madame Lila's. She is very critical, very demanding. Some of them get upset. They even cry."

"But you don't mind her strictness, do you?"

"Oh, no! I like it when she is strict with me! I know then that she gives importance to what I am doing."

That evening after supper, when they were alone in the living room, Laura reported this to Julia. Julia, sitting under the reading lamp with a book in her hand, put it down to listen to her. When she had finished, instead of responding, Julia lifted her book and began to read from it aloud: "What the dancer must do is create in herself an inner world that she can transmit to the audience. To create that world she must immerse herself in the story of the ballet, in the character she portrays."

Surprised, Laura asked, "What are you reading?"

Julia held up the book. Laura read the title aloud: *Basic Principles of Classic Ballet.* She went from surprise to astonishment. "Good heavens, Julia! Are you becoming an authority on ballet?"

"Hardly. But if we're going to understand Michaela, we'll have to know what makes her tick." Julia was silent for a moment. "We catch only glimpses of her — like the one you've been telling me about. So I thought it might be a good thing for me to learn something about ballet from the point of view of those who practice it. The other day, when we were at the school, I talked to Lila — that is, I listened to her. She is amazing when she talks about ballet. She's like a religious zealot. I'm sorry I never saw her at the top of her form as a prima ballerina.

In fact, I must admit, I've never paid much attention to ballet before this. I know a good deal more about opera."

"So I'm aware."

"But ballet is fascinating when you come to think of it — something so ephemeral, so fleeting and yet so compelling. It's not the music, it's not the choreography, it is not the spectacle. It's the dance and the dancer, something that is gone the moment it is accomplished."

Laura was smiling. "Lila must have been lyrical."

"Well, she was. She said that ballet symbolizes all the unattainable longings of the human soul — the human quest for the unattainable. The body is the instrument the dancer uses to strive for the attainable, and the limitations of what the body can do are the limitations that make the unattainable unattainable — the moonlit atmosphere of love and death in *Giselle,* for instance."

Laura looked at her but said nothing. Julia sat bemused, wrapped up in what she was thinking.

The next morning Laura was surprised when Michaela did not leave the apartment at her usual early hour. Instead, she lingered in the kitchen until after Julia had gone. For a fleeting moment Laura wondered: could it be that Michaela's monthly period was giving her trouble? Michaela had never indicated that this was ever the case.

But suddenly Michaela appeared at Laura's elbow and said in a soft voice, "Madame Laure, I have a letter from my maman."

Laura, seated at her desk, looked up at her. "What does she say?"

"She is trying to get passage on a plane that will bring her straight here. She says it will not be too long."

That evening Laura said to Julia, "This means, that she will probably get here a little before Christmas."

"Just before we go to the Houghtons."

Laura said Yes. She had heard the suppressed annoyance in Julia's voice. She knew that Julia had set aside the professional engagements that usually took place in the holidays. The paper she was going to present to the Modern Language Association could be read by someone else, she said.

When Laura had raised the question of housing Mrs. Souza, Julia had said that the sofa bed should certainly suffice for Michaela and her mother, at least for a few days. After all, they had to find out whether or not Mrs. Souza was going to be cooperative about Michaela's schooling with Lila. If she decided against the arrangement, what would they do?

"Oh, Julie," Laura protested, "she surely would not!"

"She will if she has some other scheme that is more to her advantage."

"Oh, darling, you must not be so negative about her! We must assume that she has Michaela's best interests at heart, even though her outlook is so narrow."

"And you," Julia retorted, "must not assume that everybody's outlook is as disinterested as your own. Don't you see? Michaela is the only capital she has. That is why she is so careful with her, why she agreed to let us bring the girl here. She's looking for a better financial opportunity."

The question had arisen: what would they do with Michaela and her mother while they were at the Houghtons? Lila said that she was closing her school for the holidays. There were engagements she had to supervise for some of her older dancers; she would not teach during this period.

Laura said, hesitating, to Julia, "Could we take them with us?"

Julia exclaimed, "Good God! You know how Mrs. Houghton reacted to Michaela. And then Mrs. Souza, too?"

Nevertheless, Laura had raised the question with Mrs. Houghton, who at the moment of Laura's phone call was being visited by Mrs. Outhwaite. Mrs. Outhwaite had cried out, delighted, "Oh, Eula, do tell them to bring Michaela! I'd love to see her! Lila has been raving about her so."

Eula had demurred. "But, Margot, her mother is here now. She would have to come also, Laura says."

"Oh, yes, yes! Of course, tell them to bring her along, too. I have plenty of room."

Julia had said, "I don't like this. But, then, I don't like having Mrs. Souza here, either. By the way, I think she and Michaela should eat by themselves. I can't stand to look at her blank face across the table every night."

It was Laura who went with Michaela to the airport to meet her mother. Seeing the spare, neat figure approaching them through the crowd, Laura was flooded by a sense of the reality of Michaela's life — her mother's ugly duckling, whom she resented yet tended with strict responsibility. Where had she got Michaela? Laura wondered. Who was the father who had endowed the child with such a different body? And where had Michaela got the sweetness of disposition that Laura had come to recognize under the awkwardness of a thwarted adolescent? Mrs. Souza had a plodding way of walking, as if determined to trudge through the difficulties in her life. Laura could not deny to herself that there was a resemblance: Michaela had that same stoic determination, even more obvious now that she was Lila's favorite pupil.

Laura saw Mrs. Souza give Michaela a close brief scrutiny as she reached them, just before she turned an unfriendly eye on herself. She returned Michaela's hesitant kiss with a dry one of her own, and said, "How do you do, Mrs. Houghton." Then they stood, the three of them, in awkward silence for several moments before Laura, taking charge, led the way out of the airport.

Mrs. Souza said, "I have a package, besides my luggage. It is being held in Customs."

"Julia will see about it," Laura replied.

In the cab Laura said, "Mrs. Souza, you are staying with us for a day or so. We thought you could share Michaela's room, since we shall be going down to Virginia for the holidays — all of us."

Mrs. Souza nodded but said nothing.

In the next few hours, when they had returned to the apartment, Laura, trying to assess Mrs. Souza's response to her new surroundings, debated whether to raise the question of Michaela's future with Lila.

In the end, that evening she said to Julia, "Let's

postpone talking to her about that until we get back from Virginia — unless she raises the question. I don't know how much Michaela has told her."

Julia agreed.

The following day, among the Christmas cards in the mail there was one from Mrs. Houghton enclosing a note. "Dear Laura," she said, "it is getting close to the time of your visit and I can't tell you how I long for you to be here. You so often came at this time of year, when Dick never did."

"Oh, God!" Laura breathed. "How shall I ever shed this burden?" She read on. "I must tell you that Catharine Ingalls has written to me, saying that she expects you will be with us at Christmas and she wants so much to join us all at that time. Laura, will that be objectionable to you? I feel I should invite her, she says she misses Dick so much."

Angrily Laura threw the letter down. She was still angry when Julia arrived home in the evening. Julia was at once aware that something had disturbed Laura's usual composure.

"What's eating you, honeybunch? You're as mad as a wet hen."

"Here, read this." Laura tossed the note to her.

Julia, having read it, slowly raised her eyes to Laura's. "I'll never understand such gall in my life."

Laura, who was standing in the middle of the living room, clasped and unclasped her hands. "What can I say? I can't tell Mother Houghton that I won't have the woman in the house while I'm there. She wouldn't expect that of me."

"Well, you could."

"What reason should I give?" When Julia did not

reply, Laura went on. "She knows Catharine only as a great admirer of Dick's. She doesn't know she was his mistress. A lot of people admired and loved Dick. They write to the Houghtons all the time and sometimes they stop by for a visit. I can't tell her the truth."

Julia made a face of disgust. "Well, we'll have to put up with her then."

Laura was silent for a moment and then made an effort to stir herself out of her anger. "I had another letter."

"Not from Catharine, for God's sake!"

"Oh, no. From Mrs. Outhwaite. She is formally inviting us to bring Michaela and her mother, who can stay with her. She says she likes to have people about her, especially in the holidays. She is most gracious."

"So she is. And Mrs. Souza will be delighted, too, I've no doubt. Mrs. Souza knows how to use wealthy people for her own ends."

"Oh, darling! Mrs. Outhwaite is not wealthy — far from it."

"Laura, dear, Mrs. Outhwaite has a fine house in the country and is a patron of the arts. That is what Mrs. Souza will see. I am sure she will ingratiate herself with Mrs. Outhwaite."

"I shall call Margot — she says I'm to call her Margot — tomorrow," said Laura decisively.

When Laura called Mrs. Outhwaite answered immediately as if the phone was at her elbow. "Oh, Laura, you have my note! Don't you think this is a splendid idea?"

"I think it is wonderful of you, Margot, but I wonder —"

"Oh, don't worry about all that! I'm sure they would enjoy spending Christmas in the country."

"Perhaps so," said Laura, dubious. "Julia and I don't like to impose on you like this. But, you see, I'm sure Mrs. Souza will not allow Michaela to come with us by herself. She would not want to be left here in New York alone."

"Why, that's understandable. And Michaela will be happier to have her mother with her after such a long separation."

"I suppose so," said Laura, more dubious than ever.

"Come, come, Laura, I think everybody will enjoy themselves here. I am planning something for the holidays. I won't tell you now what it is, because the plans are not complete. I still have to hear from several people. But I think it will come off very well."

"I really don't know how Mrs. Souza will fit in."

"Why not? She is an Englishwoman, I think you've told me, like yourself. For that matter, I can manage French very well, if that is necessary for communication —"

"Oh, that will be no problem! I simply am uncertain whether you will like her. She is not spontaneous."

"Well, Laura dear, I think I have enough spontaneity for two. So let us leave it at that. I shall expect them when you come. It takes all kinds, you know. I've dealt with most varieties of people in my life. I think I can manage Michaela's mother. I'm so fond of that child, Laura. There is something about her that appeals to me very much. And Lila tells me that she — shows such perseverance, such dedication in overcoming obstacles. That is something any artist will respond to, you know. This brings back to me all the struggles I had as a young actress — all the difficulties I had to overcome. My family did not approve of actresses and then when I was launched out on my own, I found myself in a very different world from the one I had grown up in — to say nothing of all the sexual pitfalls I encountered. Now, when all that is behind me, it is a joy to see a young life opening up in this way."

"Yes," said Laura. "I shall tell Mrs. Souza and see that they get ready to come with us."

Julia, standing beside Laura's chair, said, "I heard most of that. She still has a stage voice. Well, we'll go down in a group. It will be a job packing the car."

III

The weather was mild for the middle of December. There had been as yet no freeze, only a few light frosts that left the vegetation brown and red and the grass still green. They reached Mrs. Outhwaite's house late in the afternoon, when the short day was drawing in. Laura, sitting next to Julia who was driving, was aware that excitement had been building up in Michaela, sitting behind her. Laura had tried during the long trip from Manhattan to dispel the weight of silence by pointing out to Mrs. Souza various landmarks, aware nevertheless that Mrs. Souza paid little attention to what she said. There just isn't, she thought, any common ground for understanding between us.

She did notice that, when they arrived in the dusk at The Shrubberies, Mrs. Souza was alert and watchful, taking in the size of the house, the spacious garden, the friendly glow of lamplight in the windows. Mrs. Outhwaite was at the door to greet them, kissing Laura and Julia and hugging Michaela.

"My, you've grown tall!" she exclaimed, pushing the girl away from her to look her up and down. Then she turned to Mrs. Souza who stood at one side watching with expressionless eyes. "How do you do, Mrs. Souza. I am glad to meet Michaela's mother."

Mrs. Souza replied, "How do you do," but otherwise stood passive as if waiting for further instructions. Laura noticed that Mrs. Outhwaite several times glanced at her in an appraising way as she explained the arrangements she had made for them. "Michaela," she finished, "you know the house. Take your mother upstairs to the room you had before."

Turning to Laura she went on, as Michaela picked up her mother's bag and her own and started off toward the stairs, "I'd love for you to stop for a welcoming drink. I know that Eula is anxiously awaiting you, but you could take a little time, don't you think?"

Julia looked inquiringly at Laura, who said, "Just a short one, then."

In the living room a table near the fireplace held a silver ice-bucket and glasses and bottles and a tray of hors d'oeuvre. "Will you fix your own?" Mrs. Outhwaite suggested. Her own drink, already half-consumed, was on a side table by her own chair. She put her arm through Laura's. "Come and sit over here," she said, as Julia began to make the drinks.

As they sat down, she said, "Michaela looks splendid. She's taller, isn't she, and remarkably fit. But she seems a little subdued. I had hoped that Lila could bring her out more."

"She is more self-confident," said Laura, "but I think just now, since her mother has arrived, she is not so ebullient."

Mrs. Outhwaite looked at her questioningly.

Laura said, "We're somewhat uncertain about how Mrs. Souza feels about Michaela studying with Lila. I think Michaela is uneasy."

"Uneasy?"

"Well, you know, Julia and I have no authority over Michaela. If Mrs. Souza decides that she does not want Michaela to continue, there is nothing we can do."

Mrs. Outhwaite stared at her aghast. For several moments she was speechless. Then she exclaimed, "She can't do that! It would be criminal — utterly stupid!"

Laura sighed.

Mrs. Outhwaite continued to exclaim. "You cannot permit this, Laura! Lila will be outraged. We must not allow her to wreck Michaela's life! The girl has extraordinary talent. It is obvious that dancing is what she was born for. I cannot imagine Michaela in any other way of life. She would be merely a drudge doing anything else. And such a glorious gift! That is not only my opinion. Lila agrees with me. We're fortunate to have come upon such a talent at our age. It does not happen often."

"Yes, I know," said Laura, patiently. "I realize this must be so. Julia agrees with you wholeheartedly, and she is not often swept away by enthusiasm like this. But don't you see —?"

"I don't see at all," said Mrs. Outhwaite adamantly.

Laura persisted. "You must try to understand Mrs. Souza's point of view. She has had a pretty hard life. It is natural that she should be skeptical of anything like this. It is something she knows nothing about." But though she tried hard Laura knew that she was not succeeding in convincing Mrs. Outhwaite.

When finally they left The Shrubberies and drove back down the road to the Houghton place dark had come. As they drove into the graveled yard, Julia said, "There's somebody here."

Laura looked where she indicated and saw the small red car parked close to the house. She did not recognize it but she knew instantly that it must belong to Catharine. She said, "Catharine has got here ahead of us."

Angrily surprised Julia exclaimed, "What the devil does she think she's doing!"

"It doesn't make any difference, really," said Laura.

Fred Houghton had heard the sound of their tires on the gravel and was at the door to greet them. He was not a demonstrative man, unlike his son, but Dick had taken after him in physical appearance, and the sight of him standing in the lighted doorway sent a sudden shaft of memory through Laura. He kissed her on the cheek and shook hands with Julia. "Mother is in the living room," he said. "We have another visitor."

He's warning me, thought Laura, and walked across the hall, taking off her wrap.

A fire was alight in the fireplace and the several lamps around the room gave the scene a glow of hospitality. Mrs. Houghton was halfway across the room to reach Laura as she came in. She caught her in her arms and cried, "Oh, my dear child! How glad I am to see you! It has seemed such an age since you were here before."

She turned to greet Julia and Laura was left face to face with Catharine Ingalls. As usual whenever they met, Catharine did not look her in the eye. Her glance always passed just beyond Laura's gaze.

"Oh, hello, Laura! How are you?" Her tone was artificially bright.

"Hello, Catharine." Laura continued to walk across the room towards the group of chairs drawn up to the fire.

Catharine was about to follow her when she was stopped by Mrs. Houghton who asked, "Julia, do you know Catharine Ingalls? Catharine, this is Dr. Julia Cochrane."

"Oh, yes!" Catharine responded. "We've met, haven't we?"

"I believe so," said Julia, remembering another Christmas, in London, in Laura's flat, in a crowd of journalists, political people, and transatlantic travelers. "How are you?"

Mrs. Houghton and Laura sat on the sofa. Fred Houghton was busy with bottles and glasses at a sideboard. What might have been an awkward silence was filled with Catharine's bright chatter. Julia, watching her covertly, thought, Dick had a definite preference in women. He obviously liked them thin, fair, not too tall, and sophisticated in manner. But there the superficial resemblance between Laura and Catharine ended. Julia, wanting to detach herself from a contemplation of Catharine — since looking at her tended to exacerbate the indignation she was trying to suppress — eagerly responded to Fred Houghton's questions about life in New York. But not before she heard Catharine say, "I'm so glad you let me come here for the holidays, Mrs. Houghton. I couldn't bear the thought of spending Christmas with people who did not know Dick — especially this first Christmas since he has gone. I would have gone mad by myself."

Fred Houghton also heard her and Julia saw an angry flush in his face as he looked at his wife. Mrs. Houghton was pale and obviously distressed by Catharine's words. Fred stepped closer and said in a tight voice, "It will be better, Miss Ingalls, if we don't dwell on Dick's absence. I'm sure we all feel it, without the need for reminders."

Catharine seemed at first surprised by his statement and then, as if recollecting something, said hastily, "Of course. Forgive me."

Then there was a silence and Julia cast about in her mind for something to say. "We're a little late getting here because, you remember, we brought Michaela and her mother with us and we had to take them to The Shrubberies."

Mrs. Houghton said, dabbing at her lips, "Oh, yes. Laura has been writing to me about Michaela."

Julia went on. "Michaela is developing very quickly as a dancer. She is studying with Lila. You know Lila, don't you?"

Mrs. Houghton, who was obviously trying to focus her attention on what Julia was saying, responded, "Yes. She was here last September, when Margot had that troupe of dancers come. I was surprised by her. She had a great deal to say about ballet as an art. I had not realized before that there was so much to it."

"Oh, yes. The world is dance to Lila. I suppose one has to be an enthusiast to achieve the sort of success she has had. I find it intriguing to listen to her. She has such a passionate feeling for what a dancer must be — the very embodiment of the art."

Mrs. Houghton gazed at her with a slightly puzzled expression. "She believes that Michaela is capable of that sort of thing? Michaela seems such a stolid sort of girl. Orinda complained that she was clumsy and hard to teach."

Julia glanced quickly at Laura and saw that she was now sitting in an armchair a little way away from the fire, in preoccupied silence. Catharine, on the other hand had sat down next to Mrs. Houghton on the sofa and was talking about how different things were in Europe now with all the changes brought about by current events. Mrs. Houghton, who had never been out of Virginia, listened without comment. Throughout the rest of the evening Catharine kept up this bright flow of conversation, including everyone in what she was saying, through dinner and afterwards over coffee and liqueurs.

In their bedroom later, when Julia spoke of her, Laura, still passive, nodded. "Yes. She's very quick to adapt to circumstances. Those first remarks of hers were rather to test the water. Fortunately, Fred broke that up before she could mention the fact that she is sleeping in Dick's old room. There wasn't anywhere else to put her."

"God! I forgot about that." Julia thought back to the one glimpse she had had of Catharine in the past. Catharine had made little impression on her and that glimpse had been overlaid, through the years since, by the idea she had formed of her from Laura's statements and the gossip that surrounded Dick. In the course of the evening Julia had watched her covertly, becoming aware that Catharine was also watching her. There was no doubt of the fact that Catharine was a clever, astute woman, with a gift for ingratiating herself with people new to her. This was a natural enough tool for a woman in her line of work, a tool constantly honed by practice. Laura had said that Catharine was known for the probing interviews she conducted on television of people in public life and the skill she exercised in private life, with which she managed to project the image of herself as the recipient of special, intimate, spontaneous confidences from the people she met, without stepping beyond the safe borders of public knowledge. Julia had observed, throughout the evening, how Catharine had catered to Mrs. Houghton, not again trespassing on Mrs. Houghton's feelings, yet continuing to establish herself as a special friend. For after all, did she not so admire Dick as a professional news gatherer and commentator and adored him as that rare creature, a true friend when one was alone and in danger in foreign places, under fire and amid anarchy? She had very largely ignored Laura, monopolizing Mrs. Houghton and leaving Julia to carry on a conversation with Fred about the clash of interests between the United States and the French over farm subsidies.

Julia said now, "She's terribly jealous of you, darling."

Laura, whose mind was elsewhere, said in surprise, "Well, I suppose so. She always wanted Dick."

"Yes, and now you're the Houghtons' darling daughter. She wants to be in first place with them. Why else would she invite herself here, hurrying down to get here before you did?"

Laura turned away with a weary gesture. "She deceived herself about Dick, you know. She thought she came first with him, before anyone else. Women often deceived themselves that way about him; some men, too. He was too easy-going to disillusion them and anyway he liked the adulation. He was just lazy, too self-centered to put them right, when the atmosphere got too intense."

Julia, aware of an old jealousy flickering in her own heart, said, "Do you think you really came first with Dick?"

"No. Dick came first with Dick. He always lived in the moment. He tried not to look back or forward."

"Whoever was there at the moment was it."

"You could put it that way."

Laura's tone was offhand, disengaged. Julia, watching her, became aware that Laura was becoming subtly sexually aroused. It was Catharine's presence that has done this, thought Julia; her presence has brought back the past and its tangle of sexual rivalries. While Dick was alive the uncertainty in Laura's private life had worked on her feelings, and in a reaction that was normal for her, Laura had been prompted to clothe herself in an armor of cool composure, to quell any response that might lead to sexual awareness, in a denial of sexual stimulation. This had been a major problem for the two of them when they had first met and been attracted to each other. For a while, at the beginning, Julia had often felt repulsed and made unhappy by what seemed Laura's rejection of physical contact. Gradually she had realized that Laura's attitude had nothing to do with herself; it was Laura's way of dealing with the turmoil in her own life, caused by Dick's insecurities. She had suffered for some time, learning that Laura had disciplined herself to contain and control the effect on herself of Dick's frequent wanderings. For Dick, Julia learned, expected that whenever he returned to Laura he would be forgiven and welcomed, and that this had cost Laura a great deal of pain in welcoming and rejecting him at the same time. Laura had ceased to go to bed with him when at last she had admitted Julia to her inner life, and thereafter there had been dissension and upheaval whenever he was back in Laura's flat, until he became ill.

Now, watching the distracted nervousness with which Laura was moving about the room, Julia heard the echo of those long years. She was surprised at this result of Catharine's presence. But of course it was not just Catharine's presence. This house was the place that Laura must think of as most deeply Dick's home, the place where she had come as Dick's bride to meet his parents, even if his attachment to it had been weakened in his adult years, the place she had often visited without him to console his parents for his absence at crucial moments in their lives. Being here must cast her mind back to the time when she was young, still under the illusion of her love for Dick, still an untried wife. Julia got up from her chair. She went to where Laura was standing, lost in her own thoughts. Gently she put her arms around her. Laura turned toward her, startled, her blue eyes wide, her body tense. Has she forgotten I'm here, thought Julia, chagrined. She said softly, "Laura, Laura."

Laura suddenly vented her feelings. "Oh, Julia, she makes me so angry — so angry I can scarcely stay in the same room with her. And yet it shouldn't be Catharine who makes me angry. It is really Dick — it was Dick who betrayed the trust I put in him — the silly, childish, unthinking trust I gave him."

Julia said, angry in her turn, "It wasn't silly, childish, unthinking. It was pure and uncalculated. It was monstrous that he could not recognize it and value it."

Laura, in her arms, grew quieter. "That only makes it worse. He had no idea of what in life is truly valuable — his parents' love and pride in him, the admiration of so many people for the things he could truly do better than most." Laura leaned against Julia's more robust body as if seeking shelter. "I can't help it, darling. Her being here brings back so much I have tried hard to forget.

Why does she have to come here now? It's as if she wants to compete with me for their love and attention, as a reflection of Dick's. If that's really what she wants — to feel some of his warmth through their love, then I should feel sorry for her. I've never sought the fondness they give me. It is now a burden, which I should like to be relieved of, though I'm grateful that they feel as they do about me. After all, it is the unspoiled young Dick that they mourn. They never really knew him as a man."

Julia moved her hands over Laura's body. "But you realize, don't you, that you can't just feel sorry for her. You have to protect his parents from her. His mother especially would never accept the fact that she was Dick's mistress. If Catharine shows her real self — and in such close quarters she is bound to sooner or later — she will let your mother-in-law know what the real situation was. That would destroy what happiness she has left, to know that he was capable of deception, of deceiving everybody who loved and trusted him. He was the ideal son to her. Remember, she married late and Dick was the crowning glory of her life."

Laura said into her shoulder, "It's all so false. Yes, of course, you're right. I've kept up appearances this long for her sake — and because he begged me to, so that she would always see him as she did. I can't give up now. But you know I can't go on forever fending off Catharine."

"You'll have to do it for the length of this visit. Now, come on, let's forget it all for the time being, Laurie. Let's go to bed."

She pulled her gently toward the big four-poster and began taking off her clothes. Absentmindedly

Laura helped her and when she was naked, got in under the covers. Julia, all at once anxious, stripped off her own clothes and got in beside her. As the heat of her own desire grew, she rejoiced in the feel of Laura's soft, smooth skin, in the little throb she felt through her fingertips. They lay clasped together, sinking slowly into the state of bodily unity. The last thought that crossed Julia's mind before the reality of Laura swept everything else away was, "I was right. She wants me."

* * * * *

It was two weeks till Christmas. The December weather stayed mild. The fields around the Houghtons' house were still partly green, not yet the dun color that would come with the first real frost. There were tatters of leaves and seed pods in the verges of the roads.

"This is just what I was counting on," said Mrs. Outhwaite. "Mild weather up to Christmas — one of the benefits of this climate. I am going to have a houseful for the holidays — half a dozen people staying in my house and the rest in some bed and breakfast places in the town."

She was obviously pleased that she still had the power of attraction to bring to her the people she valued — people of the theater, people who had admired her in the days when she was a premier actress on the American stage. She was planning a production, she told Julia, "A truncated production, if you will, of the fourth scene of the fourth act of *The Winter's Tale*. As a Shakespearean, I hope you will approve of what I've done."

Mrs. Houghton said to Laura, "I don't know how Margot manages — so many guests and so many arrangements to be made and carried out. Each year I think this must be the last. But she seems to have everything at her fingertips. She thrives on the hustle and bustle. I couldn't stand the racket. Of course she has help from the local people — she is very popular with them — she brings money into the community because of the visitors she has — to say nothing of the touch of sophistication she provides."

Laura said, "She mentioned that Mrs. Souza has offered to help with the cooking and housekeeping and the sewing of costumes."

Mrs. Houghton's swiftly knitting hands paused. "Well, of course, Orinda will not tolerate any interference in the kitchen. But Margot always needs help with her stage shows."

The Shrubberies was transformed by the prospect of the holiday stage performance. Mrs. Outhwaite explained, "This is strictly an amateur show, though we do have several people from the New York stage, hopefuls who have had a taste of theatrical success. It means that the Barn must be cleaned and the stage got ready. I do expect you and Julia to come, but of course Eula and Fred won't — they never do. Come now and I will show you how we prepare things."

As they walked towards the Barn, Laura saw Michaela, half-hidden by a small tree in a big wooden tub, no doubt one of the props for the play. Mrs. Outhwaite had not noticed Michaela until she stepped out into their path. She exclaimed, "Oh, there you are, Michaela! Has Chris brought the rest of the props down out of storage? He has? Good."

She said to Laura, "We use the old loft for an attic. It is very convenient. Now I've got to see that everything is in good shape or get things repaired, if that's necessary. Mrs. Souza has offered to help me there. She is a well-trained seamstress."

She hurried into the Barn. Laura said to Michaela, still standing beside her, "Are you enjoying yourself, Michaela?"

Michaela gave her a bright glance. "Oh, yes. I've never seen a theater play set up."

"Would you like to be in it?"

Michaela gave her another fleeting glance. "Mrs. Outhwaite says I am to be a shepherdess. All I need to do is dance."

"Why, that's delightful, Michaela!"

Michaela was smiling, not looking at her. Before she had time to reply, a man's voice interrupted them. "Hi, Mickey," it said, "how about coming into town with me?"

He was a broad-shouldered young man wearing stained jeans and a checked cotton shirt with the sleeves rolled up; almost the uniform, Laura thought, of the boys in that country community. He stood partly with his back turned to her, as if tacitly excluding her from what he had to say to Michaela.

At first Michaela did not respond but merely gazed at him with no expression on her face. When he repeated his question she said quietly, "No."

"Why not?" he demanded. "I'm finished for the day. I'm not working for the old lady again till next week. Come on, let's go."

This time Michaela's reply was prompt. "No. I'd have to ask my mother."

"Ask your mother? You don't have to ask her.

139

She won't know that you've gone — she's busy in there." He gestured towards the Barn.

"No," said Michaela again, in the same firm tone.

"Oh, what the shit! You're old enough to do what you like, here, in this country. It's not like where you come from. You have to show her you can do what you like."

Michaela shook her head. "No," she said.

Laura, watching the back of his neck, saw that it had reddened under the deep tan. Cursing peevishly under his breath he abruptly turned around and flung away from them, walking rapidly toward the graveled yard where an old sports car, splashed with various bands of bright color, was parked. Michaela stood looking after him with a somber expression on her face.

When she told Julia about the incident that evening, Julia said, "That's Chris. He's the son of the Houghtons' tenant. He wasn't home when we were here with Michaela before. He still goes to the local high school but Fred Houghton pays for special technical training for him elsewhere. Fred is convinced Chris is a genius in — what do they call it? — agronomy. From what I've seen, Chris is pretty arrogant. I heard him talk back to his father yesterday. I suppose it's his age. And he'd be bound to notice Michaela."

"Do you suppose Mrs. Souza knows about this?"

"I'm sure she's alert to the possibilities. After all, fourteen is the age of experimentation."

Laura nodded. "Lila has said that she has not tried to introduce Michaela to roles that involve a male partner. She says she is not ready for that —

that a girl has to have at least minimal sexual interest to do well and that some girls are ready much sooner than others."

Julia gazed at her nonplussed for several moments. At last she said, "Of course, Lila would think like that. Ballet is the ultimate expression of the erotic in art, isn't it?"

* * * * *

The short evening brought Mrs. Outhwaite and some of her guests into the comfort of the Houghtons' lamplit living room. Mrs. Houghton sat by the tea table, which now held a decanter of whiskey, several other bottles and an ice bucket. A very tall man came into the room. The first thing notable about him after his height was the impeccable fit of his clothes. That, Julia recognized, was Bonner McIntyre, the theater and dance critic who in a career of thirty years had made himself one of the most feared men in the theater world. Even he, she thought, cannot resist Mrs. Outhwaite's invitation to come and see theater in the depths of the country. He went over to Mrs. Houghton and began talking immediately in his characteristic, clarion-clear voice.

"Ah, Mrs. Houghton, the greatest pleasure of visiting in these remote parts is renewing our acquaintance. How are you?"

When she had responded, he turned his attention at once to Julia. "Dr. Cochrane, I believe," he said. "I've had the pleasure of reading your latest book. I find feminist criticism fascinating." He gazed

141

steadfastly at her as he said this, so that she could only speculate what the hidden intent of his comment was. He went on, without waiting for her to speak, "We're in for a session of the Bard, I hear. This is an ambitious project — the whole of scene four of Act Four of *The Winter's Tale*. Quite an undertaking."

Julia said, "The heart of the play. But there are abridgements. That is one of the blessings of doing Shakespeare — he can be tailored to the occasion."

"And has been often. But she has kept the shepherds and shepherdesses, I hear."

"One shepherd and one shepherdess, to represent the rest — a truly Elizabethan tactic."

"And how about the dance of the satyrs? I should like to see that done in the Virginian countryside."

"Well, I'm afraid you won't. The satyrs dance offstage in this production."

"Ah, I see. Margot is clever. She knows how to fashion her shows to her means. And, she has a way of persuading people to help her. She has some surprising talents here who would otherwise not appear in anything but the most professional performances for love or money."

"Theatrical people do tend to be generous," said Julia.

McIntyre cocked his head at her and said to Mrs. Houghton, "I've seen your gypsy girl. I understand she is going to dance in the play. Scarcely an adequate sample of what she can do." When Mrs. Houghton did not respond, he went on, "Does she dance featly?"

Mrs. Houghton looked up at him bewildered. "Does she do what?"

"Dance featly. That is what the King of Bohemia says the shepherdess does in the play — dance gracefully," he added in a tone of kindly instruction. Seeing the look of annoyance cross Mrs. Houghton's face, he changed the subject. "A girl like that is bound to inspire the peasantry. She has a swain already, I note."

Mrs. Houghton demanded, "What do you mean?"

"The ploughboy — so Shakespearean, isn't it? He follows her about — this young man in shirt sleeves who looks like a football hero."

Fred Houghton, who was within earshot, suddenly spoke. He said hotly, "He is not a ploughboy. He is the son of my tenant. He's a serious young man. He intends to make something of himself and I intend to help him."

"Ah, yes," said McIntyre, at once more wary. "Most promising, I'm sure."

Later, when they were alone, Julia said to Laura, "Fred Houghton seems to be very touchy about the boy Chris. Did you hear him when McIntyre called Chris a ploughboy?"

Laura nodded, absently.

Julia went on. "It seems to me that Fred has put Chris in Dick's place. Don't be upset about this, darling, but I think Fred was disappointed in his son. I've watched him when his wife is talking about Dick. Not because of his public life but in his private life. When Dick left home, he really did leave home, didn't he? And then he married you, a complete stranger from another country. You didn't produce children. There is no heir. Oh, I know. Now you're the apple of Eula's eye and Fred thinks you are the perfect daughter-in-law. But he's more percipient than she is and I think he has a very good idea of what Dick's personal life was like."

Laura's preoccupation faded. "So you see him putting Chris in Dick's place."

"He's probably a bit deceived by his own longing for a son cut in his own pattern," Julia said. "But I do wonder about Michaela. It's hard to tell just how innocent she is."

"She's only fourteen," Laura objected.

"So was Juliet when she met Romeo. And so was the virgin Mary."

They looked at each other. Laura said, "Do you suppose she is in danger?"

"In danger from whom, from what? From herself?"

* * * * *

The Barn was cold and the two girls were muffled in sweaters and jogging pants. Laura, coming in from the bright, chilly afternoon into the high gloom of the great space, saw them exercising on Michaela's improvised barre. The new girl was taller and more mature than Michaela. She must be the new dancer that Lila has sent down to dance the shepherd to Michaela's shepherdess. The girl ignored Laura's entrance. In fact, she gave the impression that she was practicing alone, absorbed in herself, intent on what she was doing. She was in the midst of a plie, her heels touching, going down until her thighs were horizontal, rising again, moving one leg out in front of her and then in a circle behind her. She went on to more complicated movements, methodically rehearsing all the steps until suddenly she sprang away from the barre into a series of leaps and pirouettes.

Laura glanced at Michaela. Michaela stood motionless, with one hand on the barre, gazing transfixed at the other girl, mesmerized by the precision of her movements. How vulnerable she is now, thought Laura; unaware of herself, unprepared to fend off unfriendly attention.

The girl dancing suddenly stopped, stood still for a moment and then turned and walked back to the barre. Her whole attitude was a denial of the presence of anyone else, yet Laura caught a side glance of her eyes that showed that she was aware that someone had come into the Barn and was watching her. Realizing that Laura had noticed her slight acknowledgement, she tossed her head and turned her back.

Michaela, in an obvious turmoil of feelings, stirred herself to say, "Madame Laure, this is Denise. I am going to dance with her in the play."

Denise, busy taking off her slippers, turned a little way back toward Laura, barely enough to nod her head.

"You are the shepherd?" Laura asked.

"Oh, yes!" She put on a pair of running shoes and said as she walked past them on the way out of the Barn, "Au 'voir, madame." There was an arrogant grace to the studiedly casual bow she made to Laura before turning away.

Laura said, "She is one of your classmates at Lila's?"

Michaela, shocked, replied quickly, "Oh, no! Denise is one of the stars. She won't be with Madame Lila much longer." She paused and then added slowly, "I am upset that I am to dance with her."

"Upset? Why?"

"Because she is so much better — so much more experienced. I am very nervous. I don't think she likes it, either. She knows I am just a beginner. But it is what Madame Lila says we must do."

Trying to be encouraging, Laura said, "Denise must be a very clever dancer, since she is to take the part of a man."

"Oh, yes. She is very clever. She can imitate any of the other dancers — their ways of dancing — the gaucheries they make. She does it sometimes to make us laugh."

Julia's voice echoed in the great space. "Hello! Anybody here? Oh, there you are! Hello, Michaela."

Michaela looked up with a bright face, as if relieved to see Julia.

"You missed a rehearsal," said Laura. "Denise was here practicing. She is to be the shepherd to Michaela's shepherdess."

"I think I saw her — a thin girl running like the wind toward the house."

Michaela burst out, "Oh, yes! She has such elan — such —"

Julia looked at her. "You admire her?"

"Oh, yes! If I can ever be as good as she is —"

Julia looked her up and down. "My money is on you, Michaela."

A rare blush appeared on Michaela's face. She said hastily, "I must go and help my maman." She moved away quickly, breaking into a run as soon as she left the Barn.

"So?" said Julia.

"Poor Michaela! She doesn't think she is ready to compete with Denise. But that is probably what Lila wants — another challenge for her. I think Denise's nose is a little out of joint."

"I saw Denise talking to Catharine, who seems to have taken a fancy to her, from what she says. I'm sure she is jealous of Michaela. Denise knows that Lila has taken Michaela as her protegee and that isn't something that happens very often. Denise must be very talented herself and that means she knows what makes another dancer a threat to her. She is as much aware of Michaela's potential as Lila is. And the crowning touch: she knows that Michaela has a boyfriend."

"You mean Chris?"

"Yes."

"But does Michaela consider him a boyfriend?"

"I don't think Michaela is cut out to be celibate — especially when her adolescent juices are raging."

Laura frowned. "I'm not talking about celibacy. I'm talking about a life and death matter. Dancing is a life and death matter to Michaela."

Julia looked at her speculatively. "Maybe you're right." There was a dubious note in her voice.

* * * * *

The day of the fete dawned cold but by noon the brilliant sun had warmed the air almost to the point of mildness. Inside the Barn it was chill and the people gathering on the folding chairs that had been ranged in front of the stage were rubbing their hands together and shrugging their coat collars up

147

around their shoulders. The babble of conversation showed that most of them were old acquaintances, frequenters of Mrs. Outhwaite's summer theater.

Julia sat at the end of the first row. She had put her handbag on the seat beside her to keep it for Laura. She wondered about Catharine but when Laura appeared she was alone. There was no curtain for the stage. While the audience fidgeted in their chairs and chatted back and forth with their neighbors, the young man and woman who were to play Florizel and Perdita had mounted the stage and stood before the cardboard cottage front. A tall black man in a steep-crowned hat and a cloak, carrying a staff came forward. "Camillo, I assume," murmured Julia into Laura's ear. "Well, I suppose that costume will attest to the fact that he is a king's counsellor." The tall man rapped on the floor with his staff and said in a deep voice, "The play will proceed."

At last they reached the point when the irate King of Bohemia, taken with Perdita disguised as a shepherdess, said, "This is the prettiest low-born lass that ever 'Ran on the greensward.' "

His speech was the que for Michaela and Denise to come to the front of the stage, while the actors drew back. Julia felt a tingle of anticipation mingle with apprehension as Denise stepped forward in a bold pas de barque. Michaela, with a grace and strength that surprised Julia, sprang into the air with both feet, alighting in front of Denise. The taller girl responded by drawing herself up on her toes, catching Michaela with both hands around her waist to control her pirouette. Lila's choreography had transformed the shepherds' dance into a mime of the predicament of the disguised prince and his princess-shepherdess.

The ballet was brief, but the verve and spontaneous vigor of the two young dancers exhilarated the audience. It was obvious to Julia that Denise in the fervor of the dance had forgotten the personal antagonism she felt towards Michaela. She had a natural fluid arrogance in her movements and held her head in a triumphant stance; now she was the male dancer she impersonated. Michaela seemed to complement Denise's assertiveness in a charming acquiescence. Camillo's lines came back to Julia: "He tells her something that makes her blood look out."

There was prolonged applause before the play resumed. When the play was over and the clapping finally came to an end, the hubbub of voices rose. Mrs. Outhwaite had had trestle tables set up at the back of the Barn and now Orinda and Mrs. Souza were standing there, arranging the platters of food. A number of young people from the town were hurrying back and forth with supplies. Among them Julia saw Michaela, no longer in her shepherdess's dress, carrying a tray. She watched as Michaela passed near Denise, who stood talking to one of the male actors. She seemed to follow Michaela's movements — in surprise? Julia wondered. Or some other emotion?

Catharine emerged from the crowd and approached Denise, breaking Denise's preoccupation by placing her hand on the girl's arm. Whatever she said made Denise laugh. Julia expected Catharine to move on but instead she stayed and gradually

149

Denise's smile faded and she became absorbed in a graver conversation.

The crowd thinned as the dishes were emptied. By this time tomorrow, thought Julia, they'll all be back where they came from. She glanced around another time and saw Chris lounging against a wall scowling in the direction of Michaela.

That evening, when they were gathered in the Houghtons' living room before dinner, Catharine was especially vivacious. Her pale coloring was brightened by the exhilaration of the afternoon, overshadowing Laura. As usual, they both wore dresses — flowing, full-skirted, Catharine's with a plunging neckline, Laura's more discreetly rounded. Julia had noted, from their first evening at the Houghtons', the way Catharine glanced at her own foulard evening trousers, subtly calling attention to the difference in their styles of dress.

Catharine talked at length about Denise. "Denise was really wonderful. She's such a great dancer, so sensitive. I'm sure she will be a major star before long."

"Denise?" Mrs. Houghton asked.

"Yes, you know, the young dancer that Lila sent down here to partner Michaela. It was goodnatured of Denise to come all this way to dance with a neophyte. But, of course, she had to do it to please Lila."

"She seemed to enjoy dancing with Michaela," Julia remarked.

Fred Houghton, standing a little away from the women, seemed aware of the tension among them. He glanced at his wife, at Laura, at Julia and back at Catharine, where his gaze lingered.

"And, you know," Catharine went on, "that boy who was so taken with Michaela? He was absolutely transported by Denise. I watched him when the girls were dancing. He was one of the stage hands, you know."

"I don't think that Michaela will be worried about that," said Laura defensively.

Catharine looked at her with a smirk. "Oh, you know how they are at that age! Just the fact that a boy looks at another girl is enough to cause trouble. Ah, youth! I wouldn't put it past him to pick up and follow Denise to New York."

Fred Houghton's voice rang with indignation. "Chris has responsibilities here. He won't do anything of the sort."

Catharine opened her eyes wide at him but did not reply.

*　*　*　*　*

The snow began sifting down through the dark. There were no lights on in the house, except a dim lamp in the downstairs hall whose radiance did not extend to the windows of the living room and was only a faint glow in the glass panels at the sides of the front door. The snow fell silently, steadily, not stirred by any wind, accumulating moment by moment on the lawn, the doorstep, the windowsills, the roof, the bare branches of the trees, the tops of the boxwood. While the inhabitants slept it smothered the outlines of objects, made mysterious the familiar landscape beyond the windows.

Laura, stirring, sensed vaguely that something was happening beyond their bedroom but when she

151

listened she heard nothing, not even the usual creaks of an old house. The warmth of Julia's body reassured her but gradually the very stillness troubled her; the world seemed muffled. Getting carefully out of bed she crossed to the window and lifted the edge of the heavy curtain — Mrs. Houghton provided heavy curtains to minimize the draughts that seeped around the old window panes. Of course, snow. Snow, the all-enveloping blanket that obliterated sound and form.

Julia's voice came from the bed. "What are you doing?"

"It's snowing."

"It felt like snow all day yesterday." As Laura crawled back under the covers beside her, she asked, "Did something wake you?"

"Not really. But when I did wake there seemed to be something dangerous about. In fact, I'm uneasy and I don't really know what about."

"Something you ate — or too much eggnog?"

"No."

" 'By the pricking of my thumbs Something wicked this way comes.' We're being very Shakespearean these days. There must be something that's bothering you." Julia reached under Laura's body to circle her waist and draw her closer. "We should not let anything bother us here. The Houghtons are very fond of you and they treat me as someone they've known a long time. They are friends."

Laura pressed her face into Julia's neck. "I wish I could feel as safe as you make it seem."

"And why can't you?"

"It's not the Houghtons. I've always felt at ease

with them. Even though I feel guilty because their love for me rests on a false basis and I can't forget that."

"False?"

"My marriage — Dick's marriage. While he was alive there was always a possibility that we could resolve the situation. But he's gone now and there is no way in which I could enlighten them without crushing them."

"Perhaps that's true of Eula but I think Fred was not deceived. He may not know for certain but I am sure he has suspicions that he does not voice. He is fond of you. That is why Catharine irritates him so much. He sees in her some of the sort of artifices he recognized in his son."

Laura did not reply, but burrowed more deeply into the pillow next to Julia's head. Julia nibbled at her ear and put little kisses behind it. After a while, Julia said, "I suppose that is what's bugging you — the proximity of Catharine. You're afraid of her — afraid she is going to let the cat out of the bag — pretending innocence all the while. But what can she say that won't show herself in a bad light? She can't say you deserted Dick, because you looked after him when he was dying. What can she say?"

Laura raised her head. "She can say that I wasn't a real wife to him — that he ran after other women because I didn't give him the love he wanted —"

"That is not true!"

"She can say it and then it will be only what I say against what she says."

"Why would they believe her?"

"She can say that I'm an unnatural woman who

preferred to give you my love and that that was why his marriage became a sham and he was too noble to talk about it in the open."

Julia rose up abruptly on her elbow. "This is sickening! Don't you see how improbable this would sound? The Houghtons have known you for years — all through your marriage to Dick. Why should they listen to a stranger who suddenly comes forward with such a tale?"

Laura rolled over on her back. "Darling, she can point out that we've been close friends for years and that I've lived with you ever since Dick died. She can say that Dick never liked you. He didn't — he was jealous of you."

"But what reason would she give for telling them all this now?"

"That she doesn't want them to be deceived any longer."

"I am certain that Fred Houghton would not listen to her and he would be furious with her if she upsets his wife."

"She would not come out with it straightforwardly. She can give a hint here, a hint there. She can carry out a campaign of that sort, not just now and here, but on into the future. And she can spread her insinuations among the people who know me and know the Houghtons, so that eventually the Houghtons will begin to hear tales from other people, with all the distortions that such things accumulate."

Julia was silent for a moment. "I suppose one thing we can do is scotch the whole business by coming out with our side first."

"Our side?"

"We can say to people — to the Houghtons, if they can absorb the idea — that we have decided to live together. You're widowed. I'm not married, and we've decided to spend the rest of our lives together. The past can go hang."

Laura said softly, "I wish it could."

When daylight came the white expanse surrounding the Houghtons' house was unbroken. The snow had stopped falling but the sky at the horizon beyond the trees was a sullen grey, as if it held as much again as lay on the ground.

Breakfast for the Houghtons was a meal prepared on an electric grill that sat on a sideboard. Fred Houghton, standing beside it, asked "Bacon? Eggs?" looking from Julia to Laura.

Julia sat down to a cup of coffee and a piece of toast. Laura, sitting down next to Mrs. Houghton, accepted a cup of tea from her and waited for her egg to poach. No one expected Catharine to appear.

Fred Houghton carried his cup of coffee to the window. Presently he said, "Ah, I see Chris has the tractor out. He'll have the drive clear in a jiffy."

Julia, joining him at the window, saw the tractor with a plough attached coming slowly along the road from the farm. So, she thought, Chris did not pursue Denise to New York. That was just one of Catharine's conversational fancies. Or did Catharine inspire these things by suggesting them? Putting ideas in other people's minds?

She stayed at the window after Fred had left. Snow in the country. It was some time since she had experienced it. She was not a skier, and winter vacations were usually spent in professional activities, when she could not join Laura. She wondered now what to do with herself. Laura would undoubtedly keep Mrs. Houghton company. Catharine she wanted to avoid. A vague disquiet remained with her from Laura's talk about Catharine. She supposed Catharine might be motivated by a wish for revenge. Revenge for the many slights she had received from Dick and Laura's friends in the years when she had been the outsider to their marriage, revenge for the fact of Dick's recurrent return to Laura after the interludes with her, revenge for the last months of his life, when he had been helpless in Laura's hands and had made no effort to seek her company, her comfort. But Laura had once said that it was Catharine who would not come near him in his last illness, because she was afraid; was it AIDS? Yes, that was all understandable, given Catharine's nature. And now, according to Laura, she wanted to supplant Laura in the Houghtons' affections. But why should she think that she had any chance to do that? It was obvious to Julia that the Houghtons were the sort of people who would react to her as an intruder, a marriage-wrecker. But, Laura said, if she can convince them that it was not Dick who scuttled our marriage but I — I as a woman with a perverted nature that Dick had discovered and, being loyal, had outwardly condoned. Because, after all, these were old-fashioned people who did not question the paramountcy of marriage vows.

Shaking off her thoughts, Julia decided to go out and test the snow. In the entry at the back of the house there was a collection of rubber boots in one corner. She chose out a pair that would fit and, wrapped in her heavy coat, stepped out into the chill, damp air. There was not much possibility of a walk; the snow was too deep. Chris's tractor had cleared the graveled yard and the drive down to the road. While she debated whether to venture in that direction, Mrs. Outhwaite's car came down the road and turned into the drive. Seeing her, Mrs. Outhwaite waved enthusiastically.

"Oh, Julia! What fun! Don't you like traipsing around in the snow? It's so dramatic, isn't it? Such a transformation of the humdrum. Chris cleared my driveway, so I just had to come and see Eula."

Julia trudged across the packed snow to stand by her car. "Quite a surprise."

"That makes it all the better. It just missed my theater party, didn't it? You know, I always have good fortune that way."

"It would have been a pity to spoil that. Especially the dance."

"Ah, I'm so sorry that Lila could not come." Mrs. Outhwaite still sat in her car, making no move to get out. "I think she would have been delighted with Michaela. I do wish the child was more open. She seems so withdrawn for a girl her age."

"That's probably the result of being taken from pillar to post by her mother, don't you think?"

Mrs. Outhwaite cast up her hand in indignation. "Her mother! What a blight that woman is! I really wonder that the child is as normal as she is. You and Laura found her somewhere in France, didn't you?"

"Laura, really. Laura is extremely sensitive to people who suffer from some sort of deprivation."

Mrs. Outhwaite looked at her speculatively. "You and Laura have been friends for a long time, haven't you? Then you must know all about that terrible

157

marriage. You know, in the theater world we hear a good deal of gossip about anyone who becomes well-known in any way. Dick Houghton was very well-known to a lot of people. He had a wonderful way of seducing you even if he had no sexual interest in you or whether you were man or woman. You know, of course, that he was bisexual? If he hadn't drunk so much — that is after all a common failing — nobody would have seen the wrong side of him, except his wife — and I suppose his mistress."

Julia said noncommittally, "I was aware of the situation."

"And now they're both here." Mrs. Outhwaite at last began to ready herself to get out of the car. "Well, I won't disguise from you how surprised I was when Catharine Ingalls arrived here. I had not met her before but I heard quite a lot about her, following him all over the world — just accidentally turning up wherever he was on assignment. She seemed to be able to arrange her own assignments to coincide. Wherever she was there were tales about how unsatisfactory a wife Laura was — how eager he was to be somewhere else rather than London. These tales were spread by Catharine; everyone knew that, though it always seemed as if they came from someone else. Of course, I did not know any of this firsthand. I heard it from friends of Laura's and friends of theirs. When I moved here — I bought this house ten years ago, when I decided that it was better for me to live in the country. City living was getting too much for me. At that time I did not realize that the Houghtons were Dick Houghton's parents; you never heard of them. And then I did really become concerned that some of this gossip would reach Eula. She has such an unrealistic view of the world."

"But what about Fred Houghton?"

"He does not concern himself with anything beyond the affairs of this community — in county politics and agricultural matters. What he thinks about anything beyond that I don't know."

Mrs. Outhwaite had got out of the car and was leaning on the arm Julia offered her as they walked slowly toward the house.

Julia asked, "Dick Houghton did come to visit once in a while, didn't he?"

Mrs. Outhwaite shrugged. "Once in a blue moon. After the first time when he brought Laura here as his bride, he never came with her on a proper visit. So Eula tells me. It was always Laura who came at the occasions important to his parents — Dick's birthday, his parents' wedding anniversary. I feel for Laura, trying to cover over his shortcomings. Well, here we are."

Julia helped her up the steps.

* * * * *

Mrs. Outhwaite held open house for New Year's Eve. There was a throng of people, chiefly neighbors and some from Washington. Again, Mrs. Souza helped Orinda in the kitchen and Michaela handed around trays to the guests. Mrs. Outhwaite, vexed, said to Julia, "I didn't want them to do this, but I didn't want to make an issue of it. Mrs. Souza is a peculiar woman or at least she is outside my range of experience. She's such a mixture of subservience and stubbornness."

New Year's Day was overcast but dry. Julia and Laura returning from a post-breakfast walk, found Fred Houghton in the driveway, talking to a man dressed in overalls and a plaid jacket and rubber boots, standing by the side of a pickup truck. Houghton glanced briefly at them and said Good morning; the man touched the brim of his hat perfunctorily.

Mrs. Houghton was sitting in the living room knitting, her usual occupation. Catharine sat nearby with a half-empty coffee cup in her hand. She said, "Chris has got himself into real trouble."

Laura looked at Mrs. Houghton for explanation. Mrs. Houghton said, "There was a big dance in the town last night that ended in a brawl. They'd all had too much beer to drink. The police were called to break it up and Chris spent the rest of the night in jail. His father has come to get Fred to help. There was a lot of property damage."

"Does Chris get into this sort of trouble a lot?" asked Julia.

Mrs. Houghton answered, "He's apt to be troublesome. I have no patience with him. His parents can't control him. But Fred thinks the world of him and says all this is just because he's too big for the world he lives in. I think he needs discipline."

Julia, thinking of the limitations of life on a farm, said, "Does he want to be a farmer? Or does he want to do something else?"

Mrs. Houghton said, dismissively, "I've no idea. His father has been our tenant for a long time. Chris has grown up here. Fred has favored him ever since he was small. He intends Chris to take over

160

the farm when he is ready for it, and eventually inherit it. It is a valuable property."

Catharine struck in. "He's certainly a handsome boy. Very attractive."

Mrs. Houghton turned her head to look at her but did not reply.

That afternoon Mrs. Outhwaite came into the Houghtons' house with a flourish of cold air. Stopping to lean over and kiss Mrs. Houghton on the cheek, she said, "How are you, Julia, Laura —" she paused and glanced over at Catharine — "Catharine. You know about Chris, I'm sure. He is unscathed. He must be quicker on his feet than the others, to come out of a fight like that without a mark. Maybe prize-fighting should be his field of endeavor."

But Mrs. Houghton did not smile. "Fred is upset. He says it's unfair of the police to single Chris out for punishment when they're all to blame."

"Probably they regard him as the ringleader. Certainly he's the one the others follow."

Catharine spoke up. "Were there any girls there?"

"They all ran away before the police arrived."

"Michaela wasn't there?" Catharine persisted.

Mrs. Outhwaite shot her an impatient look. "Of course not! Her mother would not allow her to go to such a dance and I must say, I agree with her there."

"Poor Michaela." Catharine's tone was half-mocking.

Mrs. Outhwaite said indignantly, "I'm sorry for the poor child. She gets no opportunity to mingle with children her own age. Of course, it was just as well this time."

"I should think," said Catharine, "Chris would have figured out a way to take Michaela with him. He's an enterprising fellow."

"He'd have to have some cooperation from Michaela," said Mrs. Outhwaite. "She does not disobey her mother."

"That seems unnatural to me," said Catharine. "A healthy, vigorous girl like that shouldn't be so docile."

"I don't think she likes Chris that much — enough to rebel."

"He's just the sort of young male a pubescent girl finds irresistible," Catharine declared.

Mrs. Houghton intervened. "I think you have to remember that Michaela is not an American girl. She's used to doing what her mother tells her to. I'm sorry she doesn't have any boys and girls to associate with. There just isn't anybody suitable. There's only Chris. He doesn't have any sisters. And of course she doesn't go to school here."

Mrs. Outhwaite said, "All the boys were turned loose this morning. Nobody really wants them held there. The trouble is that there was considerable property damage — furniture broken up, juke boxes torn out, that sort of thing. The owner of the dance hall wants compensation. I suppose that's why Thompson came to see Fred this morning. I saw his pickup truck go by."

Mrs. Houghton said, "I'm sure Fred will give Thompson some money. I just hope he makes Chris work some of it off. It's not good for the boy to think he can go scot free."

When Mrs. Outhwaite left, Julia walked out of

the house with her. Julia said, "Do you really think that Michaela does not like Chris?"

"I'm pretty sure she doesn't. She obviously tries to avoid him. He comes to my house a lot, on some pretext or other. Orinda has noticed it. She doesn't trust him."

"Does Michaela avoid him because she is afraid of her mother?"

Mrs. Outhwaite turned her head to look at Julia. "You're not really worried about her, are you? No, I don't think it is because of her mother. Of course, she's a difficult girl to understand. But she looks sometimes, when he's around, as if he's harassing her. And she can't go to her mother for help."

"Why not?"

"Well, you know what Mrs. Souza is like. I'd say that if Michaela complained to her about Chris, she'd accuse her of leading him on."

Julia said slowly, "I suppose so."

Mrs. Outhwaite paused with her hand on the door of her car. "You know, Julia, there's another aspect of this that is beginning to bother me. When I first suggested that I could have Michaela and her mother to stay with me, I was enthusiastic. I like the girl. What bothers me now is that something may happen that will upset the apple cart. You never know what may come of a situation like this, with a teenage girl like that. I don't feel I have much control." Frowning, Mrs. Outhwaite got into her car.

When Julia returned to the house and found Laura waiting for her in the hall, she reported what Mrs. Outhwaite had said. Laura said tartly, "She need not worry so much about it. We're going back to New York very shortly."

"Is Catharine staying on here?"

"You'll have to ask Mother Houghton. I think she will try to. I don't think the Houghtons could bring themselves even to hint that a guest should leave, no matter how unwelcome she might be. Besides, Catharine plays on Mother Houghton's feelings, her grief for Dick. This annoys Fred. He wants very much for his wife to come to terms with the loss of Dick and Catharine's sort of sympathy doesn't help that."

* * * * *

Laura, standing in the window of their bedroom, looked out into the early dawn light, watching Fred Houghton ride out of the yard on his big brown horse. When the weather permitted, he often rode out at this early hour. On other visits Laura had often accompanied him. He had two or three saddle horses.

She turned back into the room and said to Julia, who sat in her dressing gown in the armchair, "Fred has just ridden out. It's the first time the weather has been nice enough. He didn't say anything to me last night about going with him."

"Would you have liked to go with him?"

"I shouldn't have wanted to."

"Why?"

"I don't feel as comfortable with him as I used to."

"Why not?"

Laura was thoughtful. "I think it is because I

164

have a feeling that Catharine has managed to arouse his suspicions about Dick's last illness — about the cause of his death."

"It was AIDS, you said."

"Yes, but Dick refused to accept it — refused to believe that he was dying and that it was AIDS he picked up somewhere. He made me promise that I would not tell his parents. I was to deny it if anybody said what it was. People say to me now that he is dead that I don't have to abide by what I promised. Some of them say it is my duty to let the world know as part of the campaign to demythologize the disease. But I can't do that. As far as I am concerned, that would be a breach of trust. Dick always relied upon what I said I should do. Trust isn't something that you honor at a whim, according to circumstances. I could have refused to give him any promise, but he would have raved. He was miserable enough without my adding to his misery."

"So you did your best to keep his parents from visiting him."

"Yes. As it happened, Mother Houghton is frightened to death of flying and of any sort of travel, really. Fred would not leave her. He did not want her to go because he knew that she had created such an illusion about Dick that seeing him would be terrible for her. In the end, remember, Dick died suddenly. He was up and down for a long while, and then it was all over in a moment. His parents thought he died of some disease he had picked up in one of the uncivilized parts of the world he visited. And what difference does it make? He is just as dead."

Julia, realizing that this was the first time that Laura had been able to unburden herself of the details of her husband's death, even to her, kept quiet.

Laura went on. "In any case, he would have refused to let them see him. Catharine has used that fact to spread stories about how possessive I was — how I isolated him from everyone, including herself. But that is not true. He would have let her see him. In fact, I think he wanted her to come and see him. But she would not come. She is frightened of death and she was frightened of him by then. It wasn't that she did not love him. She did — much more than I did by that time. She loves him now. Yes, it is true. She does. Her resentment of me is partly because she thinks I did not love him — that I acted just to thwart her. But her fear was greater. She has forgotten this and denies it even to herself."

Julia, indignant, quelled the impulse to speak out and said mildly, "I think you give her much more credit for real feeling than I think is true. She is not you. You are too forgiving."

"Of course she is not me," Laura retorted. "But you overlook something or at least there is something you do not realize. Dick has left her a dreadful legacy. She is in terror that eventually she will develop AIDS, which he will have given her."

Julia gazed at her for a long moment. "I didn't realize that. How do you know this?"

"She confessed it to me when Dick died, when she was overwrought. I really can't hate her when I think of that."

Julia, seeing the anguish in her face, said matter-of-factly, "The sooner we leave here the better. There are some things that can be better dealt with at a distance."

Laura nodded, her eyes downcast.

* * * * *

Julia, restless after a day spent in working on the syllabus she must have ready when she got back to the University, looked out through the narrow glass panel beside the front door and said, "I've a mind to go and find Michaela and talk to her. Perhaps I can find out whether she has talked to her mother about Lila's plans." She looked at Laura who nodded.

The air of the late afternoon was damp and chill. Julia pulled up the collar of her woolen jacket and settled the fur hat more firmly on her head. She enjoyed walking as a pastime as well as exercise. But just now walking was a means of working off the sense of something impending, some untoward event looming, that seemed to dog her. She tried to analyze it away. Probably it was simply the result of Laura's uneasiness about Catharine's presence; she was used to the fact that any uneasiness that Laura felt unfailingly transferred itself to her. She had hoped with Dick's death their lives would reach a calmer stretch of water, but so far that had not happened.

Presently she stopped walking and looked about her. She had come a good distance from the Houghton house, along the road that led beyond it to the farmhouse where the Thompsons lived. There was really nowhere else to walk. The snow had long gone, but the fields were full of stubble and wild growth and the verges of the road were muddy. The road in the other direction led into the town, where she did not wish to go. Halfway along to the Thompsons', of course, was the turn-off of the lane that led to The Shrubberies. Reaching this, she debated whether to turn back or carry out her intent to question Michaela. The early dark was gathering in the hedgerows and under the leafless trees. Impulsively she turned into the lane.

Reaching the house, lying low behind its sheltering bank of boxwoods, she avoided the gate and sought the path that led around the side of the house. She had learned that Margot preferred the sitting room that lay at the back, overlooking the graveled yard — a room that she had made her own by fitting it with the books, the mementoes, the photographs, the memorabilia that spoke of a long life in the theater. That's probably what draws me, thought Julia as she found her way around the corner of the house, the path closed in by the solid mass of boxwood.

The sound that interrupted her thoughts came suddenly, loud in the quietness: the blow of a fist on flesh. A male voice — Chris's voice, registered at once in Julia's mind — ordered, "Come on, you little bitch. You can't get away from me. I'll give you something to cry about if you don't —"

Stepping forward instantly and without thought beyond the shelter of the boxwood, Julia saw that she was perhaps a dozen feet from Chris's back. His hands pinned Michaela's arms to her sides, holding her against him. "You're going to come with me over there to the Barn." His head jerked in the direction of the dark bulk looming against the fading daylight

168

in the sky. His grip was so powerful that Michaela could not move, though she strained to keep her head away from his face. He released one hand to give her another slap across the face.

Enraged, Julia shouted, "Let go of her! Get away from her!" As she spoke she sprang forward toward them.

The sound of her voice coming from behind him caused him momentarily to loosen his grip on Michaela. As he half-turned his head Michaela instantly wrenched herself out of his grasp, kicking wildly at him and then fled, vanishing from Julia's sight behind another boxwood hedge.

Chris bellowed in pain and at first made as if to follow Michaela. Julia shouted, "Leave her alone! Don't touch her again!"

He turned back toward her in fury, his fists flailing. She could make no sense of the sounds he made. She prepared for the blow she saw coming: his fist reached the side of her head, cushioned by the fur hat. Stunned, she felt the jar as her body struck the ground and she waited for more blows. But none came. Had she been knocked out? Slowly she became aware of Orinda's bulk bending over her.

"Are you all right?" Orinda's question came to her from far away. "You broke something?"

With Orinda's help she sat up. Her brain slowly cleared and she took Orinda's outstretched hand to help herself up. Orinda put an arm around her to steady her, saying, "It's serious when you fall that way."

Leaning against Orinda, Julia said shakily, "I didn't fall."

Orinda said, "I know, ma'am. I saw it."

Orinda led her slowly to the kitchen door, standing open, letting a bright band of light shine out into the gathering dusk. Inside, she led her to a chair. Julia asked feebly, "Where is Michaela? Is she —"

Orinda answered, "She's all right. She ran right away — upstairs. He can't get to her there."

Rubbing her forehead to clear her thoughts, Julia asked, "Did you see what he was doing?"

"Yes, ma'am. I saw him lurking out there in the shrubbery for her when she was coming back from the Barn. He got here too late to catch her in there. Whenever that boy comes around here I watch him. He's trouble, that's what he is. Here, drink this. It'll make you feel better."

Julia said, "I know Michaela ran away. But what did he do after he hit me?"

"He ran away when he saw you didn't get up and I was at the door watching him." Orinda paused and added in an apologetic tone, "Miss Julia, I'm not brave like you. That boy could kill you with his fists."

Julia, sitting at the kitchen table, sipping the coffee, looked up at her. "I don't blame you Orinda. I guess I was foolhardy but I couldn't just let him hurt her."

"Well, he has a bad temper and he don't like to be thwarted. But I think he realized that things were getting bad for him."

"I would like to know how Michaela is. Where do you suppose she is?"

Orinda had returned to the counter where she was preparing a chicken for dinner. She said over her shoulder, "I expect she is with her mother. They are staying in that room up over the living room." She pointed in the general direction of a narrow passageway that led from the kitchen up some stairs. Orinda's own quarters were over the kitchen.

"Is this the first time he's tried to harm her?"

"This is the boldest he's been. That's probably because he knows you all are leaving soon, and he's not made any headway with the girl."

"She'll surely tell her mother about this."

"Now that I can't say. That girl is a great one for keeping her mouth shut. You notice she didn't even scream."

Mrs. Outhwaite's voice suddenly spoke from the doorway. "Who're you talking to, Orinda? What was all that shouting? Why, Julia, I didn't know you were here!"

Mrs. Outhwaite looked from one to the other of them. Orinda, her mouth pursed, appeared absorbed in what she was doing. Julia, aware that her head was beginning to throb and her neck was stiff, said, "Chris knocked me down. I am a little shaken up. You shouldn't let him come here."

"Knocked you down! What do you mean, Julia?"

"He knocked me down. I was trying to stop him from raping Michaela."

Mrs. Outhwaite stared at her and then glanced at Orinda for explanation. Orinda looked up and said, "He's been hanging around here, trying to get the girl to notice him. She makes a mistake going over to the Barn so late in the day, when nobody's around. She's over there practicing every moment she isn't busy."

Julia said, "He was trying to force her to go back to the Barn with him. She was trying to fight him."

Mrs. Outhwaite stood silent in the middle of the kitchen. Finally she said, "Are you hurt, Julia?"

"I'm sure I'm bruised but I haven't broken anything."

"I am terribly sorry," Mrs. Outhwaite said in distress.

"Well, just let's be glad I got there in time to stop him," said Julia. "She did not have a chance against him."

Mrs. Outhwaite's distress turned into anxiety. "I really don't know what to do. If something has been going on —" She turned to Orinda. "Has it Orinda? You should have told me."

Orinda wiped the last piece of chicken. "I would have, ma'am, if I knew enough to tell you. You know that girl's close-mouthed. I've tried to tell her that she can tell me if she's having trouble with Chris. He hangs about here all the time. But she won't say anything. I don't know whether she really likes him, underneath it all. I don't think I should say anything to Mrs. Souza. That might get the girl into more trouble."

Orinda's statement was fraught with unexpressed meaning which Mrs. Outhwaite understood. She nodded. "No, don't say anything to Mrs. Souza. We'll find out what Michaela may have told her."

"And in the meanwhile," Julia said, rousing herself and feeling twinges throughout her body, "I had better get back to the Houghtons'. Laura is probably wondering what has happened to me."

* * * * *

When Mrs. Outhwaite drove Julia back to the

Houghtons' house, Laura was waiting on the doorstep, where she had been hovering, anxiously peering out into the dark beyond the lights of the yard. Seeing her, Julia made a valiant effort to get out of the car with her usual briskness but failed. As she struggled to her feet, Mrs. Outhwaite seized Laura's arm and said, "She's had a fall. She'll give you the details. I want to get away without the Houghtons knowing I've been here."

Laura, alarmed, watched Julia's efforts to get out of the car. Julia said, "Just give me your hand. I'm creaking, but nothing is broken. Can we get upstairs without the Houghtons seeing me?"

They managed to walk past the open door of the living room, where Catharine sat with the Houghtons, and get up the stairs. When they reached their bedroom Julia said, "Help me get my things off. I need a hot bath." Wincing, she sat down on the edge of the bed while Laura stripped off her clothes. Laura exclaimed in dismay, "That is a dreadful bruise!"

"And I've got a big lump on my head," said Julia, carefully fingering the throbbing spot.

Laura, beside herself, demanded, "Julie, tell me what has happened. How did you get hurt like this?"

Julia hunched her shoulders under the robe Laura draped over her. "I tried to stop Chris from abusing Michaela and he knocked me down."

"Julie! At your age you must not do things like that!"

"What was I to do then — stand there and watch him rape Michaela?"

Laura stared at her. "What do you mean? Begin at the beginning."

"As you know, I walked over to Margot's house. When I got into the midst of the shrubbery I heard Chris shouting. When I got beyond the end of the hedge I saw that he had hold of Michaela. She was trying to get away from him and I suppose she was so frightened she couldn't scream. She's no match for his strength. So I shouted to him to let go of her and I started to run over to put him away — it was an instinctive thing. I startled him because he hadn't seen or heard me. Michaela saw me and when he loosened his grip she got free and kicked him — I hope where it would hurt the most — and then she ran away — disappeared. He was infuriated and swung around and hit me. I really think he wanted to kill somebody at that moment. He stunned me, so I don't know what happened after that till Orinda came out of the house to help me. She says he just ran away — scared of what he'd done, I suppose."

Laura, examining the bruises spreading on Julia's body, said in alarm, "I think we had better go to the nearest hospital and see how badly you are hurt."

Julia swore. "Absolutely not! We'd have everybody in an uproar. How do we explain what happened? Are you prepared to go to the police and have Chris charged with attempting to rape Michaela? And who is going to do the charging? Mrs. Souza? I don't think so."

"Yes, yes," said Laura, touching the bruises. "But the place on your head?"

"I'm all right. The fur hat saved me." Julia grimaced as she got up. "I'm going to have a hot bath and get dressed and go down to dinner. I'll say I walked too far and got chilled."

As Julia dressed, Laura said, "Mrs. Souza must

know what has happened. Michaela must have bruises. Her mother would notice."

"Yes, he hit her a couple of times." Julia winced as she put on her foulard evening trousers. "But, darling, I am bothered about what we should do. Do you suppose Michaela is in danger from him now? That he'll want revenge?"

Laura, trying to free her mind from its preoccupation with Julia's injuries, answered, "I should think she's safe right now. Margot and Orinda know what happened — Margot does know, doesn't she?"

"Yes, she came into the kitchen and Orinda told her."

"Well, I should think that Chris would not want to be seen about the place right now. But somebody ought to require him to make some sort of amends to her."

"But how to do that without raising a hornet's nest? Besides —. You know, darling, Orinda has known that Chris has been harassing Michaela, but she hasn't said anything to Margot or to Mrs. Souza because, she says, she wasn't sure how Michaela really felt about Chris."

"What on earth do you mean?"

"Well, a girl that age may be more attracted than she is aware of."

Laura said angrily, "So this is Michaela's fault."

"Now, don't get mad at me. You can see why Orinda might think like that. Michaela is a healthy girl with no outlet for her sexual feelings — for any feelings, for that matter."

"Except dancing," said Laura briefly.

"Well, yes, dancing. She must wear off a lot of

emotion in dancing. I've watched her. I'm sure she has fantasies, like any fourteen-year-old. That is one reason, I'm sure, why Lila is so enthralled by her. There is so much more inside Michaela than just a passion for perfection in dance routines. What is seething under the surface is almost palpable when you watch her dance."

Laura, as if she had heard only part of what Julia was saying, declared vehemently, "I don't believe that Michaela wants anything to do with Chris. I don't believe it."

Julia looked at her and said mildly, "There are other problems here, Laura. Margot is very upset about this. She wants Michaela and her mother to be gone, out of her house. And then there is Fred. I wonder how long it will be before he hears of this and what story Chris is going to tell him."

"That Michaela led him on," said Laura, tartly.

* * * * *

Fred Houghton heard about it very soon. The next afternoon, Julia, going down the stairs, saw him standing at the foot. He was waiting for her and when she greeted him, he said "Julia, will you come into my den for a minute."

She followed him down the short hall that passed beneath the stairs to the small room at the back of the house that he used as an office and that was referred to by everyone as his den. She had never been in it before. The lamp on the desk was lit, since the room did not get much daylight. She looked round curiously at the athletic and hunting trophies that lined the walls — Fred Houghton as a young man posed as the college champion, in uniform as an officer in the State National Guard during the second world war, as the captain of a team of marksmen, holding a shining statuette of a football hero.

He invited her to sit down in a big leather chair, one of two, while he busied himself with his pipe. Julia knew that he never smoked elsewhere in the house out of deference to his wife's delicate health. Julia wondered how Dick had managed on those rare occasions when he had spent twenty-four hours under his parents' roof, since he was never without a cigarette in his mouth.

Houghton sat down in the other leather armchair and said, "I've heard that you interrupted Chris yesterday evening, when he was having an argument with that Souza girl and that he accidently hit you."

Julia, surprised, nevertheless noted the blandness of this description of events. Growing angry, she said, "I'd hardly call it an argument. Yes, he knocked me down because I interfered with what he was trying to do to her."

Fred, hearing the anger in her voice, spoke quietly. "Chris says he was trying to persuade her to go down to the town with him. He says she had promised to go with him and then reneged and he was sore."

"I don't believe that can be true. He has been harassing Michaela — insisting that she go out with him and she has consistently refused. That was why he was angry. From my own observation, I would say that he is a very arrogant young man. He's not used to being turned down."

Fred was moderate in his tone. "Now, Julia, you

know how it is with young people. Girls of that age don't think about anything but boys. Chris is a vigorous young man, right at the stage when girls are most attracted to him. If she's playing hard to get, naturally she will drive him to do things he can't resist doing."

Julia, curbing her indignation, retorted, "Michaela has not been leading him on! She is not to blame. He has no business following her around when she has told him repeatedly that she does not want to go with him. Her mother does not allow her the freedom to choose her companions."

At the mention of Mrs. Souza, Julia saw a look of contempt pass over Fred's face. "Mrs. Souza is playing her own game. But if the case is what you say, why didn't the girl tell her mother about Chris?"

"For all I know, she may have," said Julia, aware that she was not sticking to the truth. "I suppose Mrs. Souza doesn't feel she has much say in this situation."

Again there was a brief look of dismissal in Fred's face. "What I want to say," he said, "is that I don't believe Chris meant any harm. He was simply overexcited."

He looked directly at Julia as he spoke, and she looked back, saying, "I'm sorry to have to tell you that I do not accept that. I was there. I came upon them by accident. If I had not intervened, he would have raped Michaela. She is no match for his strength."

She saw Fred's jaw harden. She realized that he did not want to be told the truth in plain words. And that he was used to using euphemisms when talking to women about embarrassing subjects. He did not reply for a while, evidently seeking in his mind for a way to refute what she said. She waited. Finally he said, "I don't believe he would have forgotten himself to that extent. However, I cannot argue with what you believe you saw. I think you exaggerate."

Hotly Julia rejoined, "I cannot have you make little of the girl's situation. She was in danger through no fault of her own — danger of a kind of violence that is devastating to a woman and especially to a young girl at the threshold of her life. Chris should not go unpunished for taking advantage of her. He should be made to realize that he cannot so lightly gain his own way at any girl's expense."

Now she saw that he was as angry as she was herself. He did not answer and did not look at her, but stared down at the top of his desk. What seemed to her a very long silence was finally broken when he leaned back in his chair as if he had reached a decision and said, "Certainly I shall reprimand Chris. In fact, I have talked seriously to him already. What I ask you to do now — since there has been no permanent damage done — is to let this incident go by without further discussion. He is ready to apologize to you for the injury he did to you — I hope you have recovered from it."

Aware of the soreness still in her body but recognizing that he sought amity, Julia said reluctantly, "Yes. He may apologize. But it is Michaela he should make amends to."

Fred, getting up from his chair, said decisively, "I can't make him do that."

He walked across the room to the door that

opened into the yard outside the house. He stood there a moment, calling out, "Chris, you there?"

Julia, still angry and dissatisfied, cast another glance around the room. She saw that this was the inner sanctum of a man who strove to assuage his dissatisfaction with his life's achievements by surrounding himself with the evidence of success. Her eye fell on the photograph that hung on the wall by his chair, just within the full glow of the lamp: a group of high school boys, the victorious team in a baseball game. She looked more closely at a boy standing at the end of the second row. That was Dick. There was no mistaking the nervy grin that had always made him instant friends throughout his life, friends who remained faithful to him long after he had abandoned them. She glanced once more round the room. It was indeed the only photograph of Dick to be seen.

Fred came back into the room, followed by the heavy footsteps of Chris's booted feet. When he stepped aside, Chris's bulk seemed to fill the small room. He was as tall as Fred and broadly built, obviously a boy used more to being outdoors than confined in a house, big in the shoulders with a deep chest. A ghostly thread of fear ran through Julia. How frightened Michaela must have been of him!

Fred said to him, "Chris, I have told Dr. Cochrane that you want to apologize to her."

Chris stood with his eyes lowered. He mumbled, "I'm sorry I hurt you, ma'am. I didn't mean to. You took me by surprise and I just lashed out."

"I forgive you what you did to me, Chris. I won't forgive you what you were doing to Michaela."

Chris's head jerked up and he said resentfully, "She was tempting me. She's been doing that ever since she came here."

"I think you're wrong about that," said Julia, trying to speak dispassionately. "That doesn't excuse what you did. You've no right to harass a girl like that. She's afraid of you."

Chris bit his lip. Fred intervened. "Chris has given me his word that he will be more careful in the future. All right, Chris?"

The boy, understanding something unsaid, glanced at Julia and spoke hurriedly, "I'm sorry, ma'am," and turned and went out of the room, closing the door noisily behind him.

Fred looked at Julia. "Let's be thankful you're not badly hurt. I know he is powerful and he doesn't realize yet that he has to curb his impulses."

"He could have broken my skull or my neck, I suppose. But, as you say, he didn't."

"I have great hopes for him. I admit that he has a lot to learn. He'll be through high school next June and I'm arranging for him to go to college. He's good at learning modern techniques — computers and such things. I can't contemplate the idea of his future being ruined by something like this. When he is ready I want to make him my manager in place of his father, who'll be ready to retire."

"If he knows you have these plans for him, I should think he'd be more careful how he behaves."

"Oh, he's only a boy! Any boy worth his salt has to sow a few wild oats. Better to get them over with early."

"No matter at whose expense?"

"You mean the girl. I'm sorry about her, Julia,

and truly thankful that nothing worse happened. I'll be frank with you. The sooner she and her mother leave here, the better for everybody."

* * * * *

The telephone on the bedside table gave its gentle peal. Laura picked it up. She heard Margot's voice: "Oh, Laura! How lucky! I wanted to get you or Julia. Can you — both of you — come over and talk to me sometime today? There's something I must discuss with you. I don't trust the phones in Eula's house."

Laura said Yes and rolled back in bed against Julia. "Margot wants to talk to us. This has to be about Michaela."

After lunch, while Mrs. Houghton took her nap, Laura and Julia walked as casually as they could out the side door of the house. Catharine was nowhere to be seen.

Margot was watching for them when they arrived at The Shrubberies. She led them into her sitting room and began abruptly, "I've talked to Michaela. She says Chris has been harassing her ever since before Christmas. I suppose you know that." She glanced at them and went on. "I'm sure you know Michaela better than I do. I don't understand the girl. She doesn't respond when you reach out to her." Seeing the protest in Laura's face, she cried, "Oh, dear! I don't want to misjudge her!"

Julia said, "What did she say?"

"She said that Chris has been trying to get her to go with him to that place in town where the young congregate. She keeps telling him that she can't — her mother won't let her. I asked why she was outside at that hour — almost dark, when she was supposed to be in the kitchen helping Orinda. She says that just at that time, before it is quite dark, she goes out to the Barn to practice. Orinda knows about this and doesn't object. I think Orinda is sorry for her. Well, apparently, Chris, prowling around, discovered that this was the case and has been following her. Pestering her about going with him. Yesterday he lost his temper — he's known for having a very bad temper. Julia, did he hurt you?"

"Yes, he hurt me but that is not the point. How about Michaela? I know he hit her."

"She has bruises on her face, but not a black eye."

"Fred Houghton refuses to have Chris publicly held accountable."

Margot looked aghast. "Oh, Julia, you're not going to stir things up, are you? That would do nobody any good."

"Least of all Michaela," said Julia. "Laura and I agree on that. But the injustice rankles — at least, with me. We are just to stand aside and do nothing?"

"Julia, you know that life is unjust. I have told her that she is not to go out to the Barn any more. She is to stay in the house where Orinda can keep an eye on her."

"Has her mother said anything to you? She must have noticed the bruises."

"No. And I haven't raised the subject because I don't know what Michaela has told her." Margot was silent for a moment and then burst out, "This is more than I bargained for. I am afraid I must insist that they leave here right away. I've talked to Lila. She is ready to have Michaela back."

"We'll have to consider the Houghtons," said Julia.

"I suppose so," said Margot. "I was thinking that perhaps you, Julia, could take them back to New York now if Laura has to stay."

Julia looked over at Laura, who shook her head.

Margot said, with a desperate tone in her voice, "I admit I am frightened. I have no idea what Mrs. Souza will do. She will hold me responsible for anything that happens to Michaela. After all, they are under my roof."

Laura suddenly stood up. "Where is Michaela?"

Surprised, Margot said, "Why, she should be upstairs tidying the rooms. Her mother insists that she should do the housework to pay for their board. It's not my idea. Orinda usually does what's necessary. Her niece comes in a couple of times a week to clean." Margot's tone was defensive. "I can't argue with that woman."

By the time she had finished speaking, Laura had left the room. She mounted the stairs that led to the upper floor of the old house, noting briefly the old theatrical prints that lined the wall. Reaching the landing, she called softly, "Michaela."

Almost at once Michaela appeared in the doorway of Margot's bedroom. "Madame Laure?"

Laura saw with distress the dark bruise across her face and her swollen lip. She stepped across the landing and taking Michaela by the arm led her back into the bedroom. "Michaela, I want to ask you some questions."

They stood facing each other. How tall she is

getting, thought Laura and how handsome! She said, "Michaela, Julia has told me what happened yesterday. Orinda says that Chris has been annoying you before this. Tell me, do you like him? I should hardly think so, after this." She reached up and touched the bruises on Michaela's face.

Michaela's heavy dark brows drew together. "I do not like him madame Laure. I have told him that I do not want to go with him. He thinks it is because I like somebody else. I've told him that is not so. Who else would there be? He says, somebody I know somewhere else. Madame Laure, I do not like any boys. I do not like for them to touch me. I keep away from them as much as I can."

She was staring at Laura as she spoke. Laura turned away from her stare, gazing about the room, noting the bed from which Michaela had stripped the clothes, the dainty dressing table laden with cosmetics, the scent of soap and powder that hung in the air. She looked back at Michaela. "You should have told Mrs. Outhwaite that he was bothering you. He evidently thinks you are being a coquette, because you did not complain to her or anyone. It was very lucky that Julia arrived in time to stop him."

Michaela's eyes flashed and she flushed. "I am very sorry that he hit madame Julie. Did he hurt her? Is she angry with me?"

"He hurt her, yes. But no, she's not angry with you. Why should she be angry with you? She does not blame you for what happened."

Michaela looked down and her shoulders sagged, as if in relief at what Laura said.

Laura went on, "Tell me, what have you told

your mother? She has seen those bruises on your face. You must have others." Laura looked down at the long-sleeved shirt Michaela was wearing. "What has she said about it?"

Michaela did not answer at once. Laura could see the familiar struggle Michaela always had in trying to express any deep feeling. She put her hand on Michaela's arm. "Come, tell me, what does your mother know? Have you told her that Chris has been harassing you? What does she say to you?"

Michaela slowly raised her head. "Madame Laure, I told Maman that I fell while I was practicing, that I was trying a new pas and I fell." Michaela's head dropped again. "I don't like to lie."

"She doesn't suspect anything else?"

Michaela shook her head.

"I do not believe that," Laura said, more to herself than to Michaela. "You have not told your mother what Chris did?"

Again Michaela shook her head.

"Why haven't you? Surely it is something she should know."

Michaela struggled with the difficulty of speaking plainly. "Madame Laure, Maman would not believe me. She will think that I have played the coquette with him. She would say that he would not act this way if I had not let him think I wanted him to."

Suppressing her anger Laura said through her teeth, "Ah, yes!"

Michaela looked at her in alarm. "Oh, madame Laure, you do not believe that, do you?"

"Of course not." Laura thought for a moment before she said, "Michaela, Mrs. Outhwaite is very much upset by what has happened. She is afraid of

Chris, of what he might do next. She wants you and your mother to leave here. Of course, you cannot, unless we take you back to New York. We are going to leave as soon as we can arrange it. You will be glad to be back with Lila again, won't you?"

She had expected Michaela's face to light up at this prospect. Instead, when Michaela looked up there was anguish in her eyes. She said passionately, "Madame Laure, I want so much to become a dancer — a real ballerina. It means so much to me. Madame Lila has been so kind to me. She also wants me to be a good dancer. I want to go back and learn with her. But —" Michaela's control failed and she lapsed into French, rapid French that Laura strained to follow. From what she said a stark picture emerged of a beleaguered girl striving to reconcile filial obedience with the overpowering demands of her own nature. The words tumbled out; the timbre of her voice rose till it sounded like that of a younger child. She came to an end, panting with the emotion she had released.

Laura listened, transfixed. This was the Michaela she had sought to reach, the Michaela she knew existed behind the stoical facade. Anxious to quiet Michaela's emotional turmoil, she said, "But, Michaela, don't be discouraged. Your mother will be less opposed when she sees how well you are doing with Lila. She will realize how important this is to you and to your future."

Michaela, not looking at her, shook her head. "Madame Laure, Maman does not like Madame Lila. She does not like you and madame Julie. She says I should not have anything to do with you — that you will spoil my life — that you are wicked, idle women, and if she does not prevent you from what you are doing, I will learn later when I'm older that you have ruined my life." Michaela stopped, as if ashamed of what she was saying.

Laura, grasping at Michaela's rapid, colloquial French, was silent, aware that Michaela was uneasily watching her from under her brows. Eventually Laura found her voice to say, "This is outrageous! Why does your mother say these things?"

"I don't know." For a moment Michaela seemed poised in midair. When she spoke it was to implore her, in English, "Madame Laure, I do not think these things. Maman will not listen to me when I try to tell her that they are not true. She says I am too young and naive to understand. But I do understand very well." She stopped again abruptly.

Laura reached out to touch her. She was not prepared for Michaela's instant move to embrace her, to seize her in her arms and crush her against her own body. For a moment Laura was motionless, stunned. Then, without forethought she responded to the fierce embrace, accepting with her own body the powerful surge of the girl's desire, the unpremeditated rush of sexual longing that engulfed Michaela and transmitted its warmth to her. The abandonment with which Michaela gripped her, the ever-quickening pulse of sexual urging that Laura felt mounting in the girl's body, told her that this was something that had not happened to Michaela before. Laura held on to her desperately, aware that she could not have remained on her feet except for the strength of Michaela's arms. She felt the pressure of Michaela's young, burgeoning breasts against her own softer ones, the thrust of Michaela's firm, taut stomach against the resilience of her own. At last reason returned and very slowly the vehemence of Michaela's grip began to subside.

Laura spoke softly into her ear, spontaneously using words of endearment, as if, she realized, this was Julia. Michaela released her and stood away from her in dejection, not looking at her.

Laura reached over to take hold of her arm, but before she could speak, Michaela raised her eyes, full of pleading and fear of rejection and said, "Madame Laure, I am so sorry —"

"Oh no! Oh no!" Laura spoke passionately. "There is nothing to be sorry about!"

Michaela looked down again and remained standing dejectedly before her.

Laura tightened her hold on Michaela's arm. "Dear girl, don't be so unhappy. You feel very much alone. But you do know that Julia and I love you and so does Lila. Nothing will change how we feel about you. It doesn't matter what happens." She stroked Michaela's head. "It makes me sad to see you so unhappy."

Michaela raised her head and this time her eyes showed the dawning of hope. "You don't blame me — for what I did just now? I could not help it."

"Of course I don't blame you." The thought that formed in Laura's mind was: don't do this again unless it is with someone you love very much; but she did not say it. Instead she said, "One can't always control one's feelings." Michaela's body obviously relaxed. Laura's tone and words seemed to come to her as a familiar sort of admonition, comforting in their familiarity. No doubt I sound like her mother, thought Laura.

Michaela said, "Yes, madame." Suddenly she had retreated once more behind her facade.

Laura sighed. "I must go back downstairs," she said, but as she turned away she looked again at Michaela. Michaela answered her gaze with humble, grateful eyes.

* * * * *

"Well, what happened?" Julia demanded. She and Laura were back in their own room. The drive back from The Shrubberies had passed in silence. "You've been in a fog ever since you went upstairs to talk to Michaela."

"She doesn't like boys."

"Boys generally or just Chris?"

"Both."

Julia looked at her fixedly. "There was more to it than that. Yes, I know. We — I mean everybody — were wondering whether perhaps she really was attracted to Chris. So she doesn't like him. What else?"

"She hasn't told her mother that Chris tried to force her. She says her mother would not believe that she had not been enticing him — just what I said, remember." Laura fell silent, lost again in recollection.

"There is still more to it than that."

"Yes." Laura answered her gaze. "I think I was the recipient — can you say that? — of Michaela's first romantic impulses. I mean the first resulting from emotion."

"What!"

Laura almost laughed at the expression on Julia's face. "It was simply that the pressure got too much for her. Can you imagine what it must have been like for her, these last few days? She couldn't hold her feelings in any longer, poor child. When I touched her she threw herself upon me. When you're that age and you have no outlet for the ferment inside you and you're tormented by the cruelty and indifference of the people round you and the person who should be your protection and your mainstay fails you — don't you see, you explode or you go crazy. I am glad that I was there to hold her for that moment."

"Oh, Laura, that is all true, but it is you who sparked Michaela. You, you." Julia caught her round the waist. "The way you do me. And here I am, jealous of a fourteen-year-old."

"Don't be silly," said Laura, pushing her gently away. "You've no reason to be. Let's say I am a step in Michaela's development. Julie, it was you who saved her from disaster."

"Thank God! Or the divine powers, if any exist. I am very thankful I was there. Now I have something to tell you. While you were gone, I listened to Margot's complaints. But in the midst of these she mentioned something important to us. It seems that Mrs. Souza has said to Margot that we — you and I — are a bad influence on Michaela. She says that we are a couple of well-to-do women who are amusing themselves by cultivating a girl who is too young to realize that she is only a plaything to us. We are distracting her from what she should really be doing: finding work to support

herself and her mother. It is a veiled threat, of
course; she means, we are not the sort of women
who should be allowed to have anything to do with
an adolescent girl. She says we are undermining the
girl's respect for her authority."

"That wretched woman! She has been saying this
to Michaela."

"Margot told me something else. She says that
Catharine has become Mrs. Souza's confidante — or
the other way round. Yes, that's what she said. You
know, I have wondered what Catharine does with
herself when she goes off in that noisy little car of
hers. She's gone for hours sometimes. Well, she goes
over to Margot's house, but not to see Margot.
Margot finds her in the house at any time of day.
She goes to see Mrs. Souza. They sit and talk in the
sewing room; Mrs. Souza is repairing theatrical
costumes to be used next summer. Sometimes they
go into the town or to that discount mall that is
about ten miles away on the highway."

Laura gazed at her in wonder. "Of course, that's
what it is. Catharine needs somebody to talk to and
Mother Houghton tries to discourage her. I imagine
Mrs. Souza has learned a lot about Dick and me."

Julia heard the chagrin in Laura's voice and
tried to allay it. "You're hypersensitive," she said,
but acknowledged to herself that Laura was probably
right. "Why should she want to talk about you?"

"It's her nature to stir things up. One of the
things about her that attracted Dick was that she
was always contriving situations in which people got
upset and talked about things that had best be kept
secret. Remember, she is a reporter for a TV
network and that is a highly useful skill when you

want to produce sensational stories about someone's private life. She is quite frank about it. She says in so many words that anybody who is in the news is fair game. Dick thought she was very clever at that."

"So now she wants to poison the air where you and the Houghtons are concerned."

"Yes. Since she can't supplant me with them, she wants to destroy their feeling for me. She tried her best to get Dick to divorce me, since I would not divorce him. She never understood why he would not do that." Laura thought for a moment. "Julie, I am very much afraid that she will disillusion the Houghtons about Dick — especially that he needed both men and women in his sex life. I was very naive when I married him. I soon found out about his affairs with women. Several of his friends were eager to let me know about them. But there was a sort of cloud about his affairs with men. I assumed that since he chased women he wasn't interested in men. It did not occur to me for quite a while that he had transient affairs with men wherever he found himself in the world."

"It's a wonder he didn't give you six different venereal diseases."

"I think he was careful to get cured before coming back to me. But when I waked up to what was happening, I stopped sleeping with him. It didn't seem to make any difference to him. That's not what he wanted me for."

"And now you think Catharine is enlightening Mrs. Souza about all this."

"Yes."

"And of course, that leads naturally to portraying us as deviant women. Well, to tell you the truth,

I've always been glad that I have deviated from the social role that has been forced upon women for so long. I would never have found you, if I hadn't."

* * * * *

Margot turned on the light to look at the clock on her bedside table. Lila had often suggested that it would be more sensible to have a clock with a radiant face or one that gave out a quiet little chime from time to time. But she had always spurned the idea. She hated Time, anyway, and the thought of hearing its footsteps or seeing its inexorable march through the night when she could not sleep — Oh, no, she would never sleep then.

Four o'clock. At this season there was another two hours before the crack of dawn — though in this climate it rarely made such a dramatic entrance — more likely it came by stealth as the light grew in the east beyond the trees.

She thought about getting up, but dallied under the covers. It had taken her hours to achieve sleep when she had gone to bed and now the worry that had murdered sleep returned.

Lila would say that she was obsessed. Perhaps so. She had come to feel that the very presence of Mrs. Souza in her house destroyed its peace. She had no evidence that the woman listened at doors and watched at windows, but nevertheless it was as if she was never free of her presence. It made it worse that she could not talk to anyone about it — certainly not Eula, her usual listener. Of course, there was Orinda. She knew that Orinda, who over the years had learned to read her moods and thoughts, understood very well how she felt about Mrs. Souza and indeed shared her feeling. But it was not right for her to burden Orinda with her own vapors.

And she could not possibly speak out to Eula. She was even afraid to go and see Eula in the easy, casual everyday way she was used to. Eula was not talkative but she was observant. Margot knew that Eula enjoyed listening to her rattle on about her memories of past glories, about the gossip of the present day. And there was the rub. She could not risk talking in her usual confidential, intimate style while this situation dwelt in the back of her mind. Inevitably she would let something slip out and then there would be no avoiding a full disclosure. She shuddered at the thought. The Houghtons were people who lived on in the world in which they had reached maturity, forty years ago. And Eula was adept at evading knowledge that would destroy the beliefs she clung to. About that son of hers principally. Her picture of him would be unrecognizable to anyone else. Margot wondered whether, in the very core of her being, Eula really did believe in this idealized creature but maintained her belief for the sake of her own peace of mind.

Day had finally come, filling her bedroom with its grey light. She must not be such a coward. She must go and see Eula and pretend that everything was as Eula imagined it to be.

As she dressed and ate the breakfast that Orinda set before her, she continued caught up in her musing. Orinda, noticing her absentmindedness, refrained from conversation. Usually breakfast was a lively time for both of them, as if overnight there had accumulated a store of things to be talked about. She's worried sick, thought Orinda. She's got to get rid of that woman.

Margot thought, I wish I knew more about Michaela. I think there is a grain of truth in what Fred Houghton says, that she provoked the attack — unwittingly, no doubt. Even now, just thinking about her, I can feel that animal magnetism — that's what we used to call it — that flows out of her to you whether you're male or female. She doesn't seem to be aware of it herself. But Fred is wrong if he thinks it's just the girl's sexuality rousing the boy's lust.

Her visit to Eula passed as so many others, but this time it seemed an endless ordeal. Once or twice she thought she noticed that Eula gave her a covert glance, as if aware that she was not her usual self. Doubtless my imagination, she told herself.

Julia, arriving back from a trip to the post office in town, met Margot as she came out of the house. She was surprised when Margot seized hold of her arm, and said, "Oh, Julia! Of course you're the one I must talk to. Do come with me." She pulled her over to her own car. "It's about Mrs. Souza and Michaela. I've had a call from Lila that I must tell you about."

"Oh?" said Julia, reluctantly following her.

Margot drove out of the driveway and turned toward her own house. She had not gone far when she pulled over to the side of the road and parked in a small space between two old trees.

She said, "I think this is better. Isn't it terrible when you can't feel free in your own house?"

"What is the matter?"

"I can't be sure that I can talk to you freely without being spied on by Catharine or Mrs. Souza. This is no fantasy. They are as thick as thieves and up till now I couldn't fathom why. But Lila has called me, as I said, and what she tells me is very disturbing."

Margot was beating her fists softly on the steering wheel. When Julia did not speak, she said, "You remember what I told you about Mrs. Souza's remarks concerning you and Laura. Now, don't misunderstand me, Julia. It is perfectly obvious that you and Laura are a couple. I've taken it for granted and I must say you make a very attractive couple and I wish you nothing but good. Lila's views are the same. She's an old flame of mine, you know. However, this is a matter that Catharine can use for her own ends. I'm sure you're aware of that. Laura fears her because of the Houghtons. After all, Laura has gone to great lengths to protect them from learning the truth about Dick. He was the golden boy whose image must not be tarnished. I do wonder sometimes why she bothered, but that's Laura."

Julia said calmly, "It would not be the end of the world if we publicly acknowledged what we are to each other. I do not fear Mrs. Souza's revelations."

"Ah, but you're not alone in this. If Catharine succeeds in making a scandal through the agency of Mrs. Souza, I think it would affect Laura very badly, because she has such a special relationship with Dick's parents."

"I suppose so," said Julia.

"And there is something further: that's the question of Michaela. When Lila called me it was to

warn me that Catharine was plotting real trouble.
Lila says that Denise — you remember that girl who
came down to dance with Michaela? Denise says that
Catharine made friends with her when she was
down here and since then has kept in touch with
her. Denise is surprised at this, but since Catharine
may well be able to help her when she leaves Lila,
she has responded. She wondered at first what
Catharine wanted — Denise is sophisticated enough
to wonder about people's ulterior motives in
friendship — but then she caught on to the fact that
Catharine is curious about you and Laura. Denise
took for granted the fact that you are a couple. She
is not gay herself but probably half the people she
knows are. I suppose her attitude reinforced
Catharine's suspicion. Lila says that Catharine has
told Denise that Mrs. Souza has now awakened to
this fact. Of course, that means that Catharine put
the idea into her head. But you realize why Lila is
alarmed. According to Denise, Mrs. Souza will say
that Michaela cannot continue in her school. This
will ruin all of Lila's plans for Michaela, because she
will refuse to let the girl have any further contact
with you two or Lila. Do you see —"

"Yes, I see," Julia interrupted, skeptically. "But
do you yourself think that Mrs. Souza will do that?"

"She's a stupid woman!" Margot spoke in fury.
"She can't see more than inch before her nose. She
doesn't understand that Michaela is being given a
marvelous chance for a wonderful career. All she
sees is that there is no money forthcoming right
now."

"You mean that she would simply tell us that
Michaela can't continue with her ballet lessons?"

"I suppose so. We might as well be living in the nineteenth century. I cannot believe that in this day and age we are being faced with the fear of dire consequences if we are exposed as being lesbians. It doesn't matter what she might say about me. That's all history. I would regret being ostracized by Eula, but I will not be intimidated. My life is what I have made it. But our problem is Michaela. She is a minor. You know what can be made of that."

Margot was looking at her fiercely and Julia recalled the weeks that Michaela had spent in her apartment. Even at that time, in the back of her mind, there had been the thought that Mrs. Souza, if it suited her purpose, could accuse them of corrupting a minor — as if Michaela's mere presence in their home was enough to corrupt her.

Julia said, "There is a little matter of bed and board — and the requirements of the immigration laws. Where would Mrs. Souza go with Michaela? They have nowhere to stay in this country except my apartment, unless they can find another sponsor."

"Perhaps Catharine is offering her a refuge — though it seems to me that that would be going to extremes for the sake of revenge, which is what this is all about, I suppose."

"I'll tell Laura what you've told me. She knows Catharine better than I do. In any case, we are leaving before the weekend."

Margot exclaimed, "Oh, my dear! I should be so relieved! The sooner you act the less damage Catharine can do."

Margot started the motor and turned the car back in the direction of the Houghtons' house. As

199

Julia got out of the car, she said, "As soon as you can let me know that you're leaving, I'll tell Mrs. Souza to pack her things."

* * * * *

Reporting to Laura her conversation with Margot, Julia said, "We're vulnerable, if Mrs. Souza wants to be nasty. Laura, I must admit that I've thought about this before. We don't have very sound ground to stand on. All we could do would be to withdraw our financial support. Michaela can stay on here in this country; she's here on a student's visa. But Mrs. Souza is only a visitor. She'll have to leave this country when the term of her visa is up." Even as she was speaking Julia saw with dismay the impact that her news had on Laura.

Laura did not reply. Troubled by her silence, Julia talked on, elaborating on what she had said, seeking to rouse Laura to voice disbelief, indignation, anger — anything that would serve as a bridge of communication between them. For she had instantly recognized in Laura's muteness Laura's retreat into the fastness of the despair into which she had sunk when Dick had died. Since their arrival at the Houghtons' Laura had borne up remarkably well, Julia knew, under the assault of the implied threat of Catharine's presence. But this — this new manifestation of the malice of fate — had momentarily vanquished her. Laura was far away, suddenly carried off from her into the remembered misery of her married life.

Julia gave up, seeing the uselessness of her efforts. Chilled by this shadow of a distance created between them she watched her sadly. This was how Laura had been at first. It had taken patient days and nights for her to recover her sense of herself. Michaela had become an integral part of that recovery. Now, in a moment, the new hopeful Laura was gone.

Laura was subdued throughout the evening, so much so that Catharine, Julia was aware, noticed. She spent a sleepless night, lying close to Julia who felt the tension in her body. At breakfast she was still almost silent and went back to their room immediately afterwards. Julia, making excuses to Mrs. Houghton that Laura did not feel well, followed her. Laura sat in the armchair, her head on her hand, her eyes cast down.

Julia picked up a book and sitting close to the window tried to read. An hour or so passed in utter silence. At last too restless, she got up and walked to the window and looked idly out. The scene had become familiar — the graveled yard, the driveway, the line of trees that marked the road in the distance. One of Fred Houghton's hunting dogs — they were not allowed in the house — was rooting in a clump of bushes on the edge of the yard — after a rabbit, perhaps.

All at once she saw a car turn from the road into the driveway. The flash of red contrasted with the uniform muted winter colors of the vegetation. Catharine's car. She watched it park in the graveled yard and exclaimed, "I can't believe my eyes. Mrs. Souza is getting out of Catharine's car!"

"What?" Laura raised her head and spoke as if she had heard Julia for the first time since the previous evening.

Julia said, "I said, Mrs. Souza is getting out of Catharine's car. Catharine must have brought her here."

Laura said, "What would she be coming here for?"

Julia, happy at her return from limbo, said, "Your guess is as good as mine. She's carrying a shopping bag that's full of things."

Laura came to the window to watch with her as Catharine led Mrs. Souza to the house. Presently they disappeared from view.

Laura said, "Do you suppose she has brought something to sell?"

"Something to sell? What on earth —" Julia's frown of perplexity slowly cleared as she remembered something. "Ah, that quantity of Portuguese drawn-thread work that she brought with her and I had such a hard time getting through the Customs for her. She claimed it was a personal possession but it was obvious that she meant to sell it, if she could. She must have brought it with her down here. Do you suppose she has brought it to show to Mrs. Houghton? I know she still has it because she never found a buyer for it in New York; she had no opportunity before we came down here."

"This would be one way to raise a little cash," said Laura thoughtfully.

Then they were both silent, listening to the sounds from downstairs. Dilsy must be ushering them into the living room.

Catharine's voice, sharp and carrying, came to them up the stairs. "Mrs. Houghton, Mrs. Souza has brought those things to show you that I was telling you about." Then the voices faded and they heard nothing more.

* * * * *

Catharine sat in an armchair to one side, watching with quick, bright eyes. The somber-looking woman, dressed in a dark tweed coat and skirt and white blouse buttoned to her chin, was slowly and carefully laying out on the sofa the contents of her shopping bag. The soft, wheat-colored linen adorned with drawn-thread work, was spread out on the pale blue cloth of the sofa, showing to advantage. She's clever, thought Catharine, in the way she is displaying her wares. She has had experience in gauging the interest and whims of the sort of women who find this kind of thing attractive. Yes, she has the gift of entering the eye of a prospective buyer, judging the effect of what she was doing. She must have learned these ways by long years of scratching for a living by catering to people with money to spend on luxuries she herself could not afford and probably would not want.

Mrs. Houghton was saying, "These are lovely things, Mrs. Souza. I like that blouse especially."

"They are made by the nuns, ma'am, in convents — like the sweetmeats they sell in Lisbon at Christmas time. The nuns teach poor girls how to make them. That is the way they earn money for their convents."

Hogwash, thought Catharine. That was certainly

the case once. I doubt if it is now. Those things were probably made by poor women working for the merchants who sell them to the tourists.

Since Mrs. Houghton made no motion to examine the things, Mrs. Souza said coaxingly, "Won't you look closely at these?"

Mrs. Houghton obediently leaned forward to examine the material Mrs. Souza held up for her to see.

"Yes, yes. I can see that they are exquisite."

The session went on. Catharine carefully suppressed her boredom. Finally Mrs. Houghton made a selection and agreed to the sum Mrs. Souza asked. She got up from her chair and went to a low cabinet placed against the wall opposite. Opening a drawer she searched among its contents, watched by Catharine and Mrs. Souza. Returning, she handed several bills to Mrs. Souza who scrutinized them carefully before placing them in a large purse she carried in the shopping bag. She stood up.

Mrs. Houghton looked at her in mild surprise and said, "Won't you have a cup of coffee with us?"

Mrs. Souza, whose ingratiating manner of someone displaying jewels, had vanished, did not answer.

Mrs. Houghton, distressed, urged gently, "Catharine, you will have a cup of coffee, won't you?"

"Oh, that would be very nice! Daphne, you are not in a hurry, are you?"

Reluctantly, Mrs. Souza sat down again, at the end of the sofa. Mrs. Houghton, more used to listening to others than to making conversation on her own, was obviously daunted by the silent presence of the woman seated on the sofa. Catharine, perversely enjoying the awkwardness of the moment, made no effort to promote chitchat. Dilsy brought in the refreshments and Mrs. Houghton served them. She made two or three attempts at conversation which died immediately, killed by the dead weight of Mrs. Souza's passive resistance.

Finally, Mrs. Houghton offered, "I've never been across the Atlantic, Mrs. Souza. It must be very interesting to travel as much as you have. You will be going back to New York soon, won't you? I hope you have enjoyed your stay here, though perhaps it seems too quiet and humdrum for you."

Catharine saw the expression on Mrs. Souza's face change from blankness to a stony rejection. "We are going to leave as soon as I can arrange it," she said emphatically.

Mrs. Houghton, committed to politeness in the face of any incivility, said, "I'm sure that Michaela is anxious to get back to her dancing. You must be eager for her to continue her training. Lila says she has such a brilliant future."

Mrs. Souza turned her head slightly, to look her in the face. The stoniness had changed to anger. "I must decide what my daughter is to do. I must take her away from here — from bad associations."

Mrs. Houghton, apprehensive at the sudden show of anger, protested. "Why, of course. I think Julia — Dr. Cochrane — is ready to go back to New York and you will go with her, of course."

"No!" Mrs. Souza's single word was explosive.

Mrs. Houghton's bewilderment increased. "But how will you go then?"

Mrs. Souza glanced briefly at Catharine. Catharine was gazing away from them.

Mrs. Houghton asked, "Catharine, are you taking Mrs. Souza with you to Washington?"

Catharine said hastily, "I'm afraid I can't do that. I can't put them up, you see. I have a very small apartment — an efficiency." She turned in Mrs. Souza's direction but did not look directly at her as she added, "I really do think you will have to go back to New York with Julia."

Mrs. Souza's anger obviously grew with her sense of betrayal. "I will not go with that woman. Michaela must not go near her. You yourself have told me what kind of woman she is. You should understand why we cannot go back to New York with her."

Catharine looked at Mrs. Houghton with raised eyebrows, as if to disclaim any complicity with Mrs. Souza.

Mrs. Houghton, becoming annoyed, said, "Mrs. Souza, I don't know what you mean. Dr. Cochrane is a guest in this house. I do not understand what you accuse her of. You came here with her. Why can't you go back to New York with her?"

Mrs. Souza said bitterly, "Because I know now what sort of woman she is. I did not know before. Miss Ingalls has told me."

Mrs. Houghton looked at Catharine. "What have you told her, Catharine?"

But before Catharine could answer, there was a noise at the door and Margot came hurrying into the room, saying, "Oh, Eula!" She stopped and stared first at Mrs. Souza and then at Catharine. "Orinda told me that Catharine was fetching Mrs. Souza over to show you her Portuguese pieces. I had intended to bring her myself. Why didn't you wait for me, Mrs. Souza?"

Mrs. Souza looked away from her in silence. Margot turned to Catharine, "Why were you so eager to bring her here yourself?"

Catharine tried to be casual. "I wasn't eager to, Margot. She was telling me that you had said that Mrs. Houghton wanted to see her things so I offered to bring her over. I did not know that you were going to bring her and she did not tell me."

Indignation prevented Margot from speaking at once. Mrs. Houghton asked, "But, Catharine, I want to know what you told Mrs. Souza about Julia."

Catharine shrugged. "She must have misinterpreted something I said. Since Julia is ready to return to New York, naturally Mrs. Souza must go back with her."

Mrs. Souza stood up. "I must speak to Mr. Houghton."

"What about?" Margot demanded.

Mrs. Souza looked at her, her intense dislike apparent on her face. "I must tell him what I now know about this woman. He must know what sort of woman he has in his house. He will understand why I cannot have anything more to do with her — why I cannot let my daughter associate with her." She seemed to speak without emotion, as if the anger that had motivated her first outburst had now run underground.

Mrs. Houghton looked at her in bewildered

dismay. She said to Margot, "What is she talking about? Fred has not met her. Does she want him to decide what she must do?"

Margot, aware that to Eula an appeal to Fred was the solution to any problem, said soothingly, "I don't really know, Eula. I don't see how Fred could help."

Catharine suddenly got to her feet and said to Mrs. Souza, "Since Mrs. Outhwaite is here, I'm sure she will take you back to her house. I think I had better leave you all to solve your own problems." She walked quickly out of the door to avoid being stopped.

But before she reached it, Margot, who looked as if she wanted to step in her path, exclaimed, "You are the biggest troublemaker I've ever met."

Catharine's face reddened and for a moment she hesitated, as if she was going to answer, but then decided that she did not care enough and hurried out of the room.

Mrs. Houghton, watching her go, asked Mrs. Souza, "What was it she told you?"

Mrs. Souza did not answer but looked steadily away from her. Margot, alarmed at how upset Mrs. Houghton seemed, said hastily, "I think Mrs. Souza had better come with me now." She glanced at her as she spoke and added, "You are acting in a deplorable way, Mrs. Souza. This is no way to repay the kindnesses you have received. You'd better reconsider what you intend to do. Now come with me."

Docilely, Mrs. Souza got up, ready to follow her out. Then Margot said to Mrs. Houghton, "Perhaps we'd better talk to Fred. Is he here now?"

Mrs. Houghton glanced at the mantel clock. "He's in town, at the County Council's meeting. He won't be back for another hour or so."

"Well, call me when he gets back. And try not to be too upset, dear."

* * * * *

In a rage Catharine, walking out of the living room, ran headlong up the stairs to the landing. Dashing into her room, she slammed the door shut.

Standing in the middle of the floor she silently screamed, Damn, damn, damn! Why did I bother to come here? What did I think I was going to be able to accomplish with these backward-looking, limited people? Why did I choose to come here into Laura's stronghold? She has always had the inside track — cold-hearted bitch that she is. And these stupid people. Who would have thought such people could produce Dick? They're taken in by her — always have been. They can't see beyond that sanctimonious facade — the way she talks about Dick, as if she ever really loved him and now wants to guard his memory. I asked him, I don't know how many times, how could he have fallen for her — poor, happy-go-lucky, open-hearted Dick. He was a sitting duck for anybody that put up a good show of wanting him. But he knew how to prick the bubble of other people's pious humbug, other people's vanity, other people's self-conceit. Why didn't he see through her? Why didn't he realize that she'd poisoned his parents' minds so that they thought she was his savior, his oh-so-loving wife?

She stood, shivering with fury, with loathing,

with a sense of defeat. How familiar it was. He'd not excluded Laura from the scathing, vicious witticisms he had coined at the expense of everyone he knew. He knew how to find people's weaknesses, their foibles, making fun of his closest friends, projecting the ridiculous in their most intimate moments. But people had not held this against him. Oh, sometimes there was somebody who couldn't see the brilliance of his caricatures. She had known this side of his nature better than anyone. Had seen him tear apart anyone who had in a moment of weakness confided to him some deeply felt emotion or secret fear. He had delighted her with his parodies of Laura's wifely devotion, his ridicule of the convictions that governed her behavior. The needs of the moment were always his criteria for behavior. Anyone who, like Laura, acted consistently on principle earned his mockery.

She despised Laura. She hated her fair, bland beauty, and seethed with anger whenever someone commented on the similarity of their physical appearance. Underneath the rage she dimly sensed that it had nevertheless been that resemblance that had first attracted Dick to her. Goddam Laura! She was always there in every memory of Dick, as she had always been there while he was still living.

Catharine yanked open the door of the closet and reached in to pull out dresses, slacks, blouses, throwing them recklessly into the suitcase open on the bed. What secret was it that gave Laura the power to call Dick back to her again and again? Why did he, in spite of himself, run back to her for solace, cherishing, when his inner despair got too much for him? He wouldn't stay with me then. He

210

pushed me away, as if I was part of the self-contempt that seemed regularly to overtake him.

Why did I come here? Did I really think I could find something of Dick here, where Laura was — because this was where Laura was? I was a fool to think that there would be here some assuagement for my hurt, for the ache in my soul.

She stood still for a moment and gazed about the room. Dick's room where young Dick had grown up. What a surge of joy she had felt when his mother had told her that this was his room, which she was to use. There were still mementoes of him about — a faded banner on one wall commemorating his high school graduation, some books in a small bookcase, school texts with the margins heavily inked, annotated with his adolescent comments; often she had leafed through them at night when she had left the others downstairs. But the savor of touching what his hands had touched, of reading what his young mind had composed, had evaporated quickly. These evidences of his one-time presence were poor stuff for the evocation of the Dick she had known, the Dick she yearned for.

That was the problem: the Dick she knew, the Dick who had been hers, was not the Dick known to his parents. It was Laura with whom she shared him — the same Laura who remembered the true Dick. Laura, who could now put a woman in his place, who could transfer the prize of her love to a woman —! Bitterness welled up twofold in Catharine.

She began to tremble. It was also Laura who knew the fear that gnawed at her. She glanced rapidly and desperately into the corners of the room, as if what she feared might be lurking there. It was always this way: whenever her longing for the feel of Dick's arms around her, for the ardent warmth of his body, for the reality of his thrust into her body, came to her, she felt this check, this sudden chill that turned him from a beloved into an enemy, someone from whom she must flee, from whom she should have fled when he was alive. If she had only known in time — the remembered ecstasy turned into a shuddering dread that racked her body.

In a frenzy of rage and fear she slammed shut the lid of her suitcase and viciously whipped the zipper closed. With hands shaking with the current of baffled longing that engulfed her, she shrugged on her coat, pulled the velvet hat onto her head. For one more moment she stood immobile. Oh, Dick, Dick! Then flinging open the door of the room she glanced down the stairs. There was no one there. She fled down them to the front door and out of the house.

* * * * *

Laura sat in the armchair in the bedroom, trying to focus her attention on the book in her hand. Julia had gone out to walk off her restlessness. Laura heard the sound of Catharine's rush up the stairs, the slam of her door. After a while Margot's voice reached her from the entry, saying Goodbye.

She threw down the book, a vague alarm fluttering through her, and went down the stairs and into the living room. Mrs. Houghton sat in her usual chair by the window, but her workbag had fallen to the floor beside her and her hands were idle.

Laura exclaimed, "Why, Mother Houghton, what is the matter?"

Mrs. Houghton looked up at her. "I don't know what to think."

"Is it something to do with Catharine?"

"Well, yes. She brought Mrs. Souza here to show me some Portuguese fancy work." Mrs. Houghton gestured towards the material strewn on the sofa. "Do you find it difficult to understand Mrs. Souza, Laura?"

"Understand her? No."

"Oh, I don't mean the way she speaks. Of course, you're more used to that than I am. I mean, she seems to me to be a peculiar sort of woman. She dislikes you and Julia very much. I know people are sometimes not grateful for kindnesses done them, but she seems so bitter."

"What did she say about us?"

"It's chiefly Julia she objects to. She says she will not go back to New York with her. She says Catharine has told her something about Julia and that Julia is not the kind of woman she wants anything to do with. I can't understand her attitude, after all you and Julia have done for her and her daughter."

Rage suddenly rising in her, Laura said carefully, "I'm afraid she is a narrow-minded woman who doesn't understand much that has happened to her. She tends to blame other people for her problems. She does not appreciate what a wonderful chance Michaela has in learning to dance with Lila."

Mrs. Houghton looked at her and said mildly, "To tell you the truth, Laura, I don't know that I would want a daughter of mine to be a dancer."

Laura suppressed a sigh. "But, you see, Mother Houghton, Michaela has so little opportunity to learn anything that would provide her with a satisfying life."

"If you say so, dear. Well, when I told her that I did not understand what she was talking about, she said she wanted to talk to Fred. She said he would understand why she was objecting to Julia. I told her he would not be home for a while. Margot seemed to think this was a good idea and said she would arrange to bring Mrs. Souza back here when it was convenient. Oh, dear, I do wish all this could be cleared up. Where is Julia, dear?"

Julia's voice came from the doorway. "Do I hear my name — not taken in vain, I hope? Has Catharine left for good? She was putting her suitcase into her car when I arrived just now. She seemed to be in a big hurry. She didn't speak to me."

"So quickly!" Mrs. Houghton exclaimed.

Julia eyed the material on the sofa. "Are those the things Mrs. Souza brought for you to look at?"

"Yes," said Mrs. Houghton. "Aren't they pretty?"

"You've bought them?"

"Why, yes — to please Margot, mostly."

"And when she left she took the money with her?"

Mrs. Houghton looked surprised. "Yes, of course."

* * * * *

The Houghtons were in the living room at the usual hour before the evening meal. Julia followed Laura into the room warily, her skin pricking with apprehension. Fred Houghton, at the cabinet, where the wine and spirits were kept, looked up briefly and said, "The usual, Julia?"

With some relief but still wary she said Yes. Laura had gone at once to sit beside Eula. Left alone with Fred, Julia accepted the drink he handed her.

Fred said, "Catharine won't be with us this evening. She has gone back to Washington."

"So I understand. She left rather hurriedly."

Fred glanced at her. "Yes — without saying goodbye. Rather strange behavior. My wife is upset. She thinks that perhaps she did not make Catharine feel welcome."

"That could hardly be the case."

He glanced at her again, as if he appreciated the comment. He said, "Mrs. Souza came to see me this afternoon. Margot thought it was a good idea for her to talk to me."

"Mrs. Souza? Did Margot bring her over?"

"No. Chris did." Fred smiled slightly at her surprise. "She's not on bad terms with him. She has the same view of what happened with her daughter as I do. Chris is a boy getting to be a man and he's not fully in control of his impulses. She understands that her daughter could be very provocative to him without necessarily realizing the fact. Anyway, she asked him to bring her over and he did."

"She came to complain about me, didn't she?"

"Yes. She said that she objected to the sort of person you are and that she does not want to associate with you any more nor allow her daughter to associate with you. I asked her why she had suddenly come to this conclusion, considering the fact that she had allowed you to bring her daughter to this country and to assist her herself to come here. She said that she had not known anything about you until Catharine enlightened her."

He waited for this information to settle in the air between them and then went on, "She told me — I'm being frank with you, Julia — she accused you of being an immoral woman and that I should have my eyes opened to this fact so that I would not allow you to continue to stay in my house."

He waited again but Julia did not respond.

"I told her that I did not need to be instructed about whom I should allow to stay in my house. Furthermore, I told her that she had better be careful what accusations she made against a respectable woman who was highly regarded in her own community — that she was not likely to be believed and might well damage her own reputation. She got angry and told me I was no better than you were and that I was a disgrace to my age and family. I said, that if that was the case, she had better leave my house at once, and if she made any derogatory remarks about me and my wife, I'd prosecute her for defamation of character. Of course, I would not do anything of the kind, because I don't trade in public scandals but it served to frighten her."

Julia said bitterly, "I'm sorry that you've been subjected to this."

Fred looked at her sternly. "You understand, Julia, I have nothing to say about your private affairs. My only concern is with my wife's well-being. Laura is extremely important to her happiness. I don't say that this is altogether rational, but she has transferred her love for her son to Laura. This is a fact and I believe in dealing with facts."

"Mrs. Souza said nothing about Laura?"

"No. Her attack was on you."

"Well, you realize that I make no apology for what I am. I do not disguise what I am. I regret that you have become embroiled in this situation. It is not of my making. This is Catharine's doing. Mrs. Souza would not have acted this way without her instigation."

As she spoke, Julia glanced toward the other end of the room where Laura and Eula sat close together chatting.

Fred noticed her glance and also looked in that direction. He turned back as if satisfied that their conversation was private. He asked, "Why do you think Catharine did this?"

"She is jealous of Laura — always has been."

"But my son is dead."

"She is jealous of the love you and your wife have given Laura. She sees it as a continuation of your son's love for Laura."

"Which he demonstrated very poorly," Fred said sharply.

"I did not know him. I met him a few times but he paid no attention to me. I was not important in his life."

"I doubt that you put yourself out to flatter him." Fred twirled the drink in his glass, looking down into it. "What I'd like to know from you is how soon will you be going back to New York?"

"You remember that Mrs. Souza has refused to go back with me."

"Yes. But I think I have straightened that out. When she said that, I told her that she was acting foolishly, that I understood that she and her daughter were in this country under your sponsorship and were dependent upon you. I also understood that she had no means of support except what you provided. So I advised her to return to New York with you. If she wanted to make any charges she could do so there, but I warned her that she could find herself in trouble."

Julia looked at him. He was not looking at her. So, she thought, you're making sure that this is my problem, not yours. She asked, "Did she accept what you said?"

Fred said drily, "She didn't have a choice, did she? I told her that I would do nothing to help her return to New York by any other means and that I didn't think Margot would be able to, either. In the end she agreed that she would be ready to go with you whenever you say you're leaving."

"I see," said Julia.

Later, when they were alone, she said to Laura, "All he wants is to get us off the premises. What happens next is no concern of his. He just wants to be rid of these women's quarrels and regain the peaceful routine of his household."

Laura said, "Darling, you must admit, it isn't any concern of his and I do sympathize with his wish to be rid of it. He is being very decent, really."

Julia's agreement was grudging. "I suppose he is taking a more tolerant view than I would have expected. I'm sure that Mrs. Souza made it quite plain what she was complaining about. It was clever of Catharine to influence her so that she did not implicate you."

"Yes, Catharine is very clever at that sort of thing. And Margot was right, too. She knew that Mrs. Souza would accept male authority. That is something she understands. Since Fred said all this she would acquiesce. She would never have done so if she were dealing with us." Then Laura said pensively, "Now I must make my peace with Mother Houghton."

It was agreed that they would leave in two days' time. Julia said to Laura in a grim voice, "I'm going to drive straight through. If we leave early, we'll make it before dark. I'm not stopping except when somebody needs a toilet. I've told Mrs. Souza she can make some sandwiches and put something to drink in the cooler."

"What did she say when you told her that we're leaving tomorrow?"

"She said nothing to me. It was Margot who told her to pack her things."

Eula wept as Julia packed their suitcases into the trunk of the car. She clung to Laura who patiently reassured her, promising to return before long, patting her gently and kissing her. Fred stood behind them, grave and noncommittal. When Julia returned to the front steps to say goodbye, he shook hands with her and wished her a good trip. There was nothing in his manner that gave any hint of a reserved opinion.

When they got to Margot's house, Margot was at the gate with Orinda to see them off. Mrs. Souza and Michaela stood in the driveway with their suitcases at their feet. Michaela carried these to the car for Julia to pack. There was an anxious eagerness in her face and manner that struck Laura to the heart. Several times Michaela looked at Julia as if searching her face for some encouraging sign of compassion. But Julia's face remained impassive, grimly set in a frown. It did not relax when she said goodbye to Margot. Margot, chattering nervously, made no attempt to speak to Mrs. Souza. But at the last moment she hugged Michaela and cried, "I'm so glad you are going back to Lila. You must work very hard, child."

Orinda, when Michaela impulsively kissed her, patted her and said, "You take care of yourself, honey."

* * * * *

It was a long ride made longer by the almost complete silence in which it passed. The winter-stricken Virginian countryside gave way to the congestion around cities and large towns. The cold clarity of the country morning merged into the hazy murk of more peopled places. Mrs. Souza did not speak at all. When Julia pulled into wayside rest areas, she and Michaela followed Julia and Laura into the comfort stations. They arrived in Manhattan at dusk. When Julia had parked the car in the garage space she rented, Michaela helped her unload their luggage and take it upstairs.

Laura said then, "What are we doing about a meal?"

Julia looked at her blankly. "Why, let's send for a take-out — the Chinese place around the corner."

Laura said, "I'd better tell her." When she returned from the kitchen, Julia was pouring drinks.

By the time the food arrived, Michaela had set the table for two. Julia, noticing, asked, "Did you tell her to do this?"

"No. Her mother must have told her to."

They ate almost in silence. Afterwards, going early to bed, Julia asked, "What are you doing about Michaela?"

"I'm going to see Lila. We must see what Lila can do to help us."

In bed, the light out, they sought the illusion of being alone, away from dissension caused by others. Laura said, "I'm so sorry, darling." She pressed herself against Julia, seeking to soften the tired stiffness of Julia's body.

"There's nothing to be sorry about. What we are, what we are doing, is our own affair. What bothers me is being caught in a situation where we have to accept condescension, disapproval, insults from anyone. Yes, yes, I know. It's the price we have to pay for living in the world we must live in."

"We are fortunate that Fred behaved as he did."

"You mean, we must be thankful for small mercies." Then, aware that her sharp answer had hurt Laura, she added, "Yes, of course. He was in as awkward a position as we were. I'm glad he was decent enough to help us with Mrs. Souza. Of course, he was just anxious to be rid of the lot of us. But he could have acted the bigot."

"He genuinely likes you, Julia. He just can't imagine our way of life. He doesn't like Mrs. Souza any more than you do."

Julia raised herself up on her elbow. "Laura, I

can't stand having that woman around me. She must get out of this apartment as soon as possible."

"But what about Michaela?"

"It's obvious Michaela can't stay here. We don't know how far her mother will go in accusing us of corrupting a minor."

"But she has no evidence that we've harmed Michaela!"

"You don't know what attitude public authorities would take in such a situation. I'm sorry, darling, we can't have them here."

"Julie, Michaela is here as a student. Where would she go if she left us, left Lila? She has to stay in school somehow. Lila certainly will object to her going to any other dancing school. As for Mrs. Souza, how is she going to live if she leaves us?"

Julia sank down again into the bed with a sigh. "I don't know. I'm exhausted with trying to resolve this situation."

Laura reached up to draw her close. "Then let's forget it for the moment. You're tired out, Julie. It was a very long drive." She pulled Julia's head down on her shoulder and spoke lovingly into her ear.

IV

Lila was in her small office when Laura arrived at the dance studio. As usual she was surrounded by hubbub: girls in various styles of practice clothes — big sweatshirts, jogging pants, tights — came in and out or sat on the floor looking at photographs of ballet productions, while in the background the voices of instructors and the thump of feet, with sudden bursts of piano music, came from the practice rooms. When Laura appeared in the doorway Lila jumped up to embrace her. What an amazing agility, thought Laura, overwhelmed by the scent Lila wore.

"My dear Laura! How glad I am to see you! You've brought Michaela?"

"Not with me. But she is here, at the apartment."

"Well, you solved that ridiculous situation. It is downright obscene, what that woman tried to do. But she must not interfere with Michaela." Lila sat down at her desk again, pointing to a nearby chair for Laura, and shouted to the girls surrounding her, "Out, out, all of you! I need to talk to Laura privately. Out, out, and shut the door."

Obediently the young dancers left the room, all of them nodding to Laura and eyeing her carefully. What sort of gossip, Laura wondered, had Denise spread?

Laura said, seizing the opportunity of the slight pause in the flow of Lila's words, "We've not solved the situation. Hasn't Margot told you what happened?"

"Yes, of course. Margot tells me everything, three times over. But I understood that Mr. Hougton put an end to that business."

"No. He was very helpful, but that was because he wanted to get rid of us, especially Michaela."

"Ah, yes, because of the boy Chris. Is Julia all right?"

"Yes, Julia is all right. Mrs. Souza came back with us to New York because she had no alternative. But she refuses to let Michaela come here to you."

Lila's eyes widened in disbelief. "That cannot be! She must come back to me! There is such a wealth of creative energy there! She is not just a little girl who wants to dance." Lila paused. The trace of melancholy in Laura's manner had caught her eye. "What is the problem?"

"We are at an impasse. Mrs. Souza accuses us, Julia and me, of being immoral women who will corrupt her daughter, if she does not act to prevent this. Sending Michaela here to your school is part of our plot. But on the other hand, she is penniless and can't leave us and take Michaela with her. She hasn't put this into words but her implied threat is that she will go to whatever authorities are in charge of abused children."

Lila exploded. "What nonsense is this? The woman must be raving!"

"Unfortunately, no one who encounters Mrs. Souza would consider her to be raving," said Laura tartly.

Lila leaned back in her chair, her fiery indignation replaced by a sudden calculation. Her glance played on Laura's face; her voice was satirical. "So you are dangerous to the young? I would never have thought it of you and Julia —" there was affectionate mockery in her tone — "two such respectable women, one even a widow. Now, in the old days, when Margot and I were young —" Lila's expression changed in a flash. Sudden suspicion of professional jealousy looked out of her eyes. "Is there somebody who is prompting her to do this — some enemy of mine?"

"No, I'm sure that is not the case. I don't really know what her motivation is. Julia thinks that she is afraid of losing control of Michaela, because she sees Michaela as the breadwinner for both of them."

"Ah!" The cloud over Lila's face cleared. "Or as

bait for a well-to-do son-in-law. I know the type. But I am not giving up Michaela. Now you must sit tight, Laura, while I think of what can be done. Can you send Michaela here in the meanwhile?"

"No. She would have to disobey her mother and I don't think she will do that."

"Not even to dance?"

Uncertain, Laura said, "No."

* * * * *

A new routine established itself. Mrs. Souza was never in the same room as Julia. All her dealings, at arm's length, were with Laura. Without discussion, she undertook the preparation of meals. Laura provided her with a weekly sum for household expenses. She set Michaela to do the housework. On most days she went out for hours at a time.

"Where does she go?" Laura asked Julia.

"Maybe she is looking for a job. She can't get one legally, and where would she go to find one? I suppose there are agencies that recruit aliens as domestics."

"Perhaps she goes to the shops."

"She wouldn't be able to buy anything." A sudden thought crossed Julia's mind. "You give her money to buy food, don't you? Perhaps she pads the bills."

"She accounts for every penny. She insists on doing so."

When Laura invaded the kitchen to speak to her, Mrs. Souza made a point of standing stiffly in the middle of the room, for the most part mute. Laura would willingly have prepared the meals herself but she realized that she must allow Mrs. Souza some space in which to act. Mrs. Souza being Mrs. Souza, the semblance of an orderly household had to be maintained. Though the fact irritated her, Laura knew that she and Mrs. Souza understood each other very well, chiefly without the need for speech. So long as she and Michaela were prisoners in Julia's apartment, Mrs. Souza's wordless communication went, Laura would have to provide some occupation for her, obviously as cook and housekeeper.

Julia chafed at the arrangement. "You realize, don't you, that to all intents and purposes we are illegally hiring her? She doesn't get a wage but she gets board and lodging. I hate this. The whole thing is false."

Mrs. Souza, when she went out, did not take Michaela with her. Most of the time, except when she was doing the bedmaking and vacuuming, Michaela stayed in the room she shared with her mother. Perhaps, thought Laura, this is what her mother has told her to do. A weight pressed on Laura's spirits which she could not shake off. It was a reflection of Michaela's obviously crushed spirits. Michaela no longer responded with bright eyes and hopeful smiles when she was spoken to. When she was in her room there was never a sound of any kind.

Then Laura became aware that in the afternoons she was alone in the apartment. At noonday Michaela set out a lunch for Laura on the corner of the dining room table — a sandwich and a pot of tea. Thereafter, while Laura was immersed in what she was doing, Michaela apparently crept silently out of the front door.

Laura complained to Julia in the evening. "Why does she do this? And what is she doing out until four o'clock in the afternoon? That is when she comes back, usually after her mother is already home."

"Then her mother knows she goes out like this."

"She must. But what does a girl that age do? She has no money."

"Unless she turns tricks in the street," Julia interposed, cynically.

Laura looked at her in horror. "Oh, Julia! Surely not!" The remembrance of Michaela's frantic embrace came back to her — Michaela who did not like boys.

Julia recanted. "Of course not. But, you know, that is not too far out a thing for a girl like that to do in this city. No, I'm sure her mother wouldn't allow that, even for the sake of the money. Besides, she doesn't have the proper clothes from what I've observed."

"Oh, Julia! In fact, she needs new clothes, badly. Her shoes are a disgrace."

"Why don't you give her some money and tell her to go and get some?"

"I'm sure she would not go and do that on her own. She would give it to her mother and who knows what she would do with it?"

"Then you tell her that she's to tell her mother that you say she must have new clothes. By the way, have you ever asked Michaela what her mother does when she goes out all day?"

"Yes. She says her mother goes out in the morning to buy food and household things. That I knew. In the afternoons, Michaela says her mother likes to go to the big shops and see fashion shows and such. She says her mother loves to see wealthy, well-dressed women and imagine herself as a maid to someone like that — mind you, not to be one herself — she doesn't aspire to that — but to live in a wealthy woman's house and enjoy the luxuries of that style of living. Michaela was rather shy when she was telling me this. She explained it carefully by saying that her mother had been used to such a nice way of living when she was younger."

Julia, watching the look of pity on Laura's face, said sharply, "It's too bad she can't find that kind of life for herself — if she just wouldn't spoil things for Michaela."

"You just don't like her and therefore you don't give her the benefit of mitigating circumstances. Of course she's limited in her outlook. And I admit she doesn't seem to have any real motherly feeling for her child."

"As a matter of fact, she'd like to be rid of her."

"But she looks after her according to her own lights. I think perhaps she is taking out her resentment against her husband on her daughter. It is pitiful, really."

Julia exclaimed in exasperation. "You'd find excuses for the devil himself! Laura, the woman is our mortal enemy!"

Laura did not answer.

But she did as Julia suggested and the next time she gave Mrs. Souza household money, she added an extra sum and said that this was to buy clothes for Michaela. Mrs. Souza stood for a moment with the bills in her hand but said nothing before folding them and putting them in her apron pocket. The next day Michaela appeared in a new skirt and blouse and shoes, silently self-conscious. They've been bought in a bargain basement somewhere, Laura noted in chagrin; I wonder what she did with the rest of the money; she has put it away for a future use, I suppose.

Laura was surprised, a day or so later, when the phone rang, to hear Lila's voice. "When are you coming to see me again?" she demanded.

"Why, I was waiting to hear from you."

"Well, something has to be done about new dancing slippers for Michaela."

"What?"

"New dancing slippers for Michaela. The ones she has are in tatters and I haven't any more to lend her."

"But what do you mean, Lila? Has Michaela been going to you?"

Lila's chuckle was knowing. "So she didn't let you know? She turned up here a week ago. She didn't think I saw her; she hung around out of the way just watching. So I gave her some practice things and told her to do some exercises on the barre. I thought she was going to faint. I told her she could come every day, whenever she could. She looked very unhappy and said that her mother would not allow her to do that, that her mother had forbidden her to come here, but she just couldn't stay away. So then I thought, ah ha; maybe something could be done about that. I told her that if she would come and look after the little ones the way she used to, I'd pay her a few dollars. Wouldn't her mother like that? She looked frightened to death but next day she came and said that her mother said she could do that. There was no mention of practicing. I see to it that she gets a couple of hours a day."

"Oh, Lila! How kind of you!"

Lila said briskly, "I'm looking after my own. I have plans for Michaela. Now, I don't want a lecture from Julia about the fact that I'm hiring someone illegally. This is not anybody's business but yours and mine. Come and see me. I want to talk to you."

When Laura reported this to Julia that evening, Julia said dubiously, "In for a penny, in for a pound. I wonder where this is going to end?"

The next day, when she went to the dance studio, Laura found Lila in the midst of a greater than usual hubbub. When finally they were able to talk, Lila said, "I have so little time now. I am planning for the climax of our spring season and there do not seem to be hours enough in the day. I know. I am told by everyone that I am carrying too much, that I should drop my class for the little ones. After all, these little girls are not here for any serious purpose — only to gratify their mothers' vanity. Oh, of course, by some miracle I might discover a gem amongst them but I don't expect that to happen again in my lifetime. If I did not have them, half my time would be free."

"Then why do you keep them?" Laura asked.

"To be blunt, because they bring in money. Teaching dancing is not the road to wealth. I need the money they bring in. And there is another thing: their mothers bolster my prestige. They are flattered by my attention and they talk about Lila; they boast about having Lila to teach their little darlings. That is why, at least once or twice a week we have a

231

social gathering for them upstairs, with refreshments, a sort of morning club, so to speak, where they can talk about their girls — and many other things in the world of dance. It is amazing the gossip they exchange; I learn a great deal I would not otherwise hear. These affairs are very popular. You should attend one of them."

Laura laughed. "Perhaps I shall."

"And," said Lila, "there is another reason for keeping this going. Mrs. Rudolph — you remember, it is Mrs. Rudolph who is interested in Michaela — she loves to come here and watch the little girls and chat with their mothers. She sees them all as little darlings, little angels. She's never had children, so has not been introduced to that reality. I don't disillusion her. In fact, I indulge her. I make all these little darlings behave like little angels when she comes here. She would be very unhappy if I discontinued the class and the social thing. I do not want to make Mrs. Rudolph unhappy. She is much too valuable to me. She is generous in providing scholarships for girls like Denise and Michaela."

Lila broke off and seemed to be mulling something over in her mind. Finally she said, "What I chiefly want to talk to you about is the program I have for the spring season. I have arranged for a group of my girls to join a ballet company — it is a young company, just starting out — for a program of ballet in a theater — a small theater. It will give them the feel of what it is like to be on a stage, to appear before a real audience, as a company. It will be a combination of my girls and the dancers of the company. I do not have the twenty-two dancers that are necessary: it is *Les Sylphides* that they will dance. Yes, that old warhorse, but ideal for my purpose. Chopin's music is romantic. There is no story for the dancers to interpret — just simple, heartfelt, innocent emotions, such as teenage girls so often feel, a dreamy fantasy. There is only one male dancer; the dance company will provide him. It will give me a chance to show off my girls."

Lila stopped speaking and sat in silent thought. Laura waited. Then Lila went on, "I have arranged that the two principal dancers — the two who dance first with the young man — are to be mine. I intend to use Denise for one. Denise is very high and mighty these days. She is popular and she is in demand. She thinks she can call the tune. But she will do as I say. Michaela will be the other one — " Lila paused at the surprise in Laura's face — "yes, Michaela."

"But, Lila, can she do this?"

Lila took no notice of her question. "She will need intensive training, between now and then. But I am convinced that she will respond as I want her to."

"But what about her mother?"

A steely look came into Lila's eyes. "I will manage Mrs. Souza. But I need your help."

"Mrs. Souza certainly will not do anything I might ask her to."

"No, but you must see that Michaela stands up to her. You must give her courage."

That evening, talking to Julia, Laura said, "How on earth am I to do that?"

"You'll have to find a way," said Julia.

In the days that followed there was, to Laura's sensitive nerves, a distinct difference in the

233

atmosphere in the apartment. Small changes occurred. The first time Michaela left in the morning, after breakfast, to go to the dance studio, her mother went with her. Mrs. Souza returned by herself at noon, and it was she who set out Laura's lunch on the dining room table. When Michaela returned late in the afternoon, she hurriedly finished the housework she had left undone in the morning, in time to serve dinner.

This happened several days in a row. Laura wondered, What does Mrs. Souza do there? Presumably she went to the dance studio to see what Michaela did, to act as chaperone, perhaps, Laura thought wryly. Laura wondered how Lila would take this. But then one morning Mrs. Souza — Laura tried, as she had on other occasions, to think of her as Daphne — did not leave with Michaela. Instead she left in the middle of the morning, and Laura noticed that she wore a new dress and spring coat and hat — she's really quite smart, she thought. And then it dawned on her that this was the use to which Daphne had put the money left over from buying Michaela's new clothes. But where was she going to display this finery?

Thereafter Mrs. Souza did not accompany Michaela and sometimes she did not go out until later in the day, when she was obviously not going to the dance studio. But once or twice a week she left in midmorning, dressed in her new clothes.

* * * * *

Laura sat at her desk, absorbed in what she was doing. Vaguely she was aware that Mrs. Souza —

Daphne — who did not move with the same stealth as Michaela, had gone out of the front door. At first she did not pay attention to the noise that intruded into her thought and then she realized that it was the sound of the vacuum cleaner. Michaela must still be in the apartment.

She got up abruptly and went in search of her. She found her in the dining room. Michaela, seeing her, turned off the vacuum cleaner and waited for her to speak.

Laura said, "Michaela, why aren't you at the studio?"

Michaela, looking down at the floor, said, "Madame Lila told me to stay at home this morning and rest. I have to rehearse with Denise this afternoon."

"Well, in that case, you shouldn't be doing this. Put the thing away and come and talk to me."

As she went back to sit at her desk Laura thought, with a sudden rush of awareness, that this was the first time in what seemed a very long period that she had dealt directly with Michaela. Without being fully conscious of the fact, she had, during the last weeks, felt a void in her daily life, as if Michaela had been truly absent, as if in exile.

Michaela came into the room and sat down in the chair Laura pointed to. The familiar sense of inchoate intimacy that had been a part of their communication came back to her, with a bittersweet taste.

"Michaela, what does your mother have to say now about your dancing, now that you are back with Lila?"

Michaela looked startled, as if she had not

expected such a question. "Oh, madame Laure, Maman does not say anything."

"She does know that you practice every day and that Lila is planning for you to take part with the other girls in the ballet performance in the spring?"

"Oh, yes."

"Has she given her consent?"

Anxiety appeared in Michaela's face. She said uncertainly, "I do not know if she approves. She has not forbidden me to do this."

Poor girl, thought Laura. She is probably waiting from day to day for the axe to fall. Then she thought, with a sudden chill: Will Daphne wait till the last moment to say that Michaela cannot take part in the performance?

Laura asked, "Has she agreed with Lila that you are to dance in the ballet?"

Michaela, obviously miserable, answered, "I don't know, madame." Then she added, with a tentative hopefulness, "Maman likes very much to be hostess for Madame Lila. She likes to talk to the ladies who come to the school, the mothers of the little ones."

"Hostess! What do you mean?"

"Madame Lila has little parties for these ladies. When Maman came to the studio to see what I was doing, she saw that Madame Lila needed someone to manage things — to arrange the tables and introduce people. Madame Laure, my maman knows how to do this very well. She understands how these things should be arranged. She has had experience dealing with ladies who have money." Michaela gazed at Laura with a visible pride in this skill of her mother's.

Laura, disconcerted, said, "Then does this mean that your mother wants you to continue with Lila?"

"She wants me to go on looking after the little ones, because Madame Lila pays me. Madame Lila is very pleased with Maman. The ladies like her — even Mrs. Rudolph, who comes often. Maman tries especially to please Mrs. Rudolph. There is now a waiting list for the dancing class for little girls."

Laura contemplated her for a moment. "But that does not tell me whether your mother has agreed to let you go on as a dancer. Is Lila sure that she will not forbid you to dance at the last moment?"

This threat was obviously in Michaela's mind, hung as a dark cloud in the back of her consciousness. But she put a brave face on the situation. "Maman will not want to quarrel with Madame Lila, who pays her to be hostess. Maman knows that she would not be able to find anywhere else to work."

Laura was silent, noting the unconscious cynicism in Michaela's words. Finally, speaking slowly as she searched for words, Laura said, "You know, you must not let your mother interfere with what is being done for you, Michaela. Lila is counting on you. Mrs. Rudolph is putting up the money for your scholarship. These are not things that you can throw away for any reason." Laura thought, Here I am, preaching rebellion.

Michaela listened to her in silence, not looking at her. When Laura finished speaking, she continued to sit mute for a while. Just as Laura was about to give up expecting her to respond, she suddenly raised her eyes to look directly at her. Her gaze was intense, brooding, as she said, "Madame Laure, I am now a dancer. I am just a beginner but I know that I will always be a dancer. It is dance that means life to me — how can I say it? I don't know the words. Dance owns me. I cannot get away from it. Madame Laure, can you understand?"

She made a move as if to reach out and grasp Laura's arm but checked herself. The two of them hung in space together, seated two feet apart yet conjoined in intimacy. Finally Laura was able to say, "Yes, yes, I do understand! Oh, Michaela, you cannot say No to something that is right inside you — something that possesses you. It would be a denial of yourself, if you do not do what this instinct tells you to do."

She heard her own words as weak and inexpressive of the emotion Michaela had aroused, but Michaela seemed satisfied. She said simply, "I will stay with Madame Lila, if she does not send me away."

"She will never do that!" Laura exclaimed.

Michaela's brooding eyes dwelt on hers but she did not respond. Laura, trying to find words of encouragement, said, "I am sorry that your mother does not understand. But you have friends who do, who realize that you have talent that should not be wasted."

Again it seemed to Laura that what she said fell far short of what she wanted to convey. Michaela continued to gaze at her, now with a trace of preoccupation in her eyes, as if her own situation absorbed more of her attention. Laura, watching, thought, She isn't the child I knew. She is leaving childhood behind, and she knows this.

Michaela said, "Madame Lila says that I may come and live with her if I need to. She will always have a place for me. But Maman would not allow that."

In spite of herself Laura's voice held contempt. "She is a very selfish woman."

"She is my maman," said Michaela humbly.

* * * * *

The days that followed had, to Laura's sensitive nerves, a strange quality. It was as if she and Julia were witnesses of a drama in which they seemed to have no part and yet which would ultimately affect their future. Laura noticed that Julia, every evening when they were at home, played the stereo set, seeking serenity in the music of Bach; this was something she had come to recognize over the years as Julia's response to prolonged episodes of stress.

Laura also observed that Mrs. Souza — Daphne, she reminded herself — was away from the apartment more and more. She was always there in time to prepare dinner, but otherwise she seemed to be engaged in something that took up more and more of her time. When Laura mentioned this, Julia made no comment.

Laura said, "I don't want to ask Michaela questions about her mother. She seems to have settled into a regular routine of practicing. So she's all right. I've not been going to the studio because

Lila is in such a turmoil. She is pressed on all sides — training her dancers, rehearsing the choreography, dealing with the notices about the performance. I can't get a moment's rational conversation with her."

Julia nodded.

The evening came when Laura, returning with Julia from an afternoon spent at a colloquium on Shakespeare's women, was aware as she stepped into the apartment that there was a stillness. At this hour there were usually faint sounds from the kitchen and the aroma of dinner preparing was in the air. She had wondered, while they were on their way home, whether Mrs. Souza would be annoyed by their lateness; she had learned that Mrs. Souza liked punctuality.

"Isn't she here?" Laura asked, anxiously.

Julia, who had not noticed anything unusual, said, "Why, I suppose she is. We didn't tell her we wouldn't be home for dinner."

Laura started for the kitchen but suddenly Michaela stood in the doorway — how tall she is! Laura exclaimed to herself: she's as tall as Julia.

Michaela came into the living room. She said hurriedly, looking from one to the other of them, "Madame Julie, madame Laure, Maman is not here this evening. She said I was to tell you but you have been out." She seemed fearful, as if expecting an angry response.

Julia and Laura exchanged glances. Julia asked, "Well, where is she?"

Michaela explained in a rush. "Mrs. Rudolph is giving a dinner party and she wanted Maman to come and prepare food and see that it is served properly."

Julia looked indignantly at Laura. "Well, of all the —" She broke off and said to Michaela, "Was this a sudden arrangement? Has Mrs. Rudolph been hiring your mother for this sort of thing?"

Michaela quailed before Julia's sternness, but she said eagerly, "Oh, madame Julie, Maman is so anxious to please Mrs. Rudolph. Mrs. Rudolph does not have a good housekeeper. She needs Maman. Maman did not want to disappoint her. There wasn't time —"

Julia cut her short. "Never mind. Your mother is free to do what she wants. But she should have let us know ahead of time."

Michaela still stood, dejected. She looked pleadingly at Laura. "Madame Laure, Maman said I was to prepare the dinner, but I can't. I do not understand her instructions."

Julia looked at Laura. "You'd better handle this," she said, retreating to the other end of the living room.

Laura said, walking toward the kitchen, "Come, Michaela, you can help me."

Julia insisted that Michaela eat with them. Less apprehensive now, Michaela, eating hungrily, answered her questions eagerly. Yes, she practiced many hours every day, even in the mornings. Madame Lila said she did not need to spend so much time with the little ones. Madame Lila was very strict; she made the dancers learn to understand the music, the choreography. It was very exciting; soon they would have a rehearsal with the dancers from the ballet company. Michaela's eyes glowed as she spoke.

Julia looked at Laura again, and said to Michaela, "And what about your mother? Is she at the studio while you are there? Does she watch you? Does she know what you are doing?"

There was a noticeable drop in Michaela's enthusiasm. "No, madame, Maman does not come to the studio unless Mrs. Rudolph is there. She is busy with a lot of things for Mrs. Rudolph. She goes to shops. She arranges the tea parties for Mrs. Rudolph. Mrs. Rudolph likes to play cards. She has friends who come to play with her often and she likes to have Maman take care of things."

"Mrs. Rudolph pays her for this?"

"Oh, yes."

"And how about Lila? Does Lila know about this?"

"Oh, yes. Madame Lila likes Maman to do things for Mrs. Rudolph. She is glad that Mrs. Rudolph likes Maman so much."

Julia looked at Laura once more and said, "Well, it takes all kinds, doesn't it?"

The next day Laura, reaching Lila by phone through the cloud of uproar that surrounded her, heard her say, in answer to her questions, "Oh, yes. Miriam thinks she is a jewel."

"But," Laura objected, "does she realize what Mrs. Souza's status is as an alien?"

"Of course. Miriam understands the situation very well. She is taking a gamble, just as I am, though for another purpose. More than a year ago Miriam lost the housekeeper who had been with her for thirty years; the woman died. Miriam was devastated. The woman was much more to her than a housekeeper. Since then she has been very unhappy. She is used to having someone with her who is absolutely competent, absolutely faithful. She thinks she has found her in Mrs. Souza. Amazing, isn't it? I suppose we all have gifts, if only they can be uncovered. I think Mrs. Souza will probably tell you very soon that she is leaving you."

"But, Lila, what about Michaela?"

Lila, half exasperated, said, "Michaela is all right. Do you think I am any less concerned about her than you are?"

"Is she ready for this performance?"

"She may be a little ragged in her technique. She is only now beginning to acquire polish. But the essence of her future will be in this; it will show through to the audience. I am convinced of this. Right now she is like a sponge. She does not resist her teacher. This will change. She will rebel. Her own will must dominate eventually. Now she is still learning to conquer the physical demands of dance. This performance will open a new way for her." Lila paused and Laura heard the note of speculation in her voice when she went on. "Perhaps we shall see something of the future Michaela in this *Sylphides*."

"But, Lila, what about her mother. What will you do if Mrs. Souza takes Michaela away?"

"Mrs. Souza will have nothing to say about the matter. Miriam will tell her that she must consent to Michaela's continuing with me. Mrs. Souza will not defy Miriam. She's not that stupid."

Lila paused and then said, "The dance company is going on tour right after this performance. Michaela is going with them."

"Does Mrs. Souza know this?"

"I've no idea. I haven't told her but I assume Miriam has."

She was silent for a moment, letting this bit of information sink in. Laura said, "How is Mrs. Rudolph going to legalize Mrs. Souza's status in this country?"

"I don't know. That's not one of my problems, thank God. I must hang up now, Laura."

Julia said, when Laura reported this conversation, "But it is ours. We brought the woman here."

* * * * *

The evening was fair and the sky still a violet glow as they rode in the cab to the theater. The same question was in both their minds: Was Mrs. Souza going to be in the audience?

Julia broke the silence by asking, "Have you ever met Mrs. Rudolph?"

"Yes, once, when she was at the midmorning social gathering I attended at the studio. She is a small woman with rosy cheeks — I suppose there's some rouge there. She is very friendly; she likes to pat you while she is talking to you. But I think she is very shrewd; she looks at you sharply. I'd say it would be difficult to deceive her."

The theater was small, as Lila had said. The foyer was already noisy with the throng that filled it. When they found their seats, in the front row, they found themselves next to Mrs. Rudolph, splendid in satin and brilliant jewels, and accompanied by a large party. Laura scrutinized it; there was no sign of Mrs. Souza — Daphne.

Mrs. Rudolph greeted her affectionately and smiled while she looked Julia up and down when Laura introduced her. Obviously observing Laura's searching glance, she said, "Mrs. Souza did not come. She does not care for ballet, and she said she had too much to do to get ready for travel. We're leaving for Paris in the morning. I shall be away for the summer in Europe."

She turned away before Laura could say anything else.

Les Sylphides was in the second half of the program, the last of the evening's offerings. When the curtain went up on the empty stage, Julia saw that the background was of painted panels, representing a woodland glade; no positive images of trees but a general backdrop evoking a forest setting. When the corps de ballet ran onto the stage Julia's eyes sought Michaela. She recognized her at the end of one wing of dancers. Opposite, on the end of the other wing, was Denise, immediately recognizable by the swift grace with which she separated herself from the other dancers and moved forward with the sole male dancer to the center of the stage. Michaela's timing was a moment late — undoubtedly the result of hesitation on her part as she unconsciously sought to follow Denise. But the moment's hesitation was lost at once as she moved into the next figure of the dance which required her to balance Denise in the trio.

Absorbed, Julia watched as the three dancers performed a pas de trois and then blended again with the corps. Denise's performance compared to the rest was brilliant; her slender, elegant body flowed through the maneuvers required of her. Laura, remembering the day in Margot's Barn, watching Denise practice before Michaela's eyes, saw again the polished ease, the artful perfection of her movements. Would Michaela's sturdier body ever achieve that sort of effortless grace, she wondered.

But as the ballet continued, Julia, watching intently, saw something else begin to emerge in Michaela's dancing. The girl was obviously rapt; she had become the dance she was executing. There was some strength here, some inner fire, that, in spite of small mistakes, challenged the greater perfection of training of the other girls. As she watched her, Julia became aware that there were moments when Michaela created the shadow of an illusion that she was lighter, taller, more slender than in fact she was. She was amazingly quick, agile, sure of herself: whatever vision she had of the essence of the dance glowed behind her movements. In their rotation of roles, she seemed to soar beyond Denise. Lila had said that this ballet had no story; the characters were undefined. That was the way Denise was dancing it, a lovely doll capturing the admiration of the audience.

But Michaela — there was a hint of mime in the way Michaela danced. The girl she represented slowly became unique, distinct among the other dancers from whom first she separated herself and then with whom she once more blended. Julia thought: this is what Lila had seen from the beginning, the promise of something unusual — Michaela holding a vision of psychic energy, of truth and beauty — a vision that, when she matured, she would present so powerfully that she could

246

overwhelm those who saw her dance, to whom she would give the vicarious experience of enjoying her own emotional strength.

Yes, this is what Lila had recognized. Lila had said: I have saved her from a type of training that might have distorted her young body, and then I would have had to retrain her. I was trained that way when I was a child: to suppress emotion, eliminate all expression of my own personality. The ballet was everything and the dancers only skillful mannequins. The discipline was terrible — terrible on young bones and psyches. I had to unlearn this. I have saved Michaela from that. Discipline, yes. The classical Russians, you know, insisted on having very young children to train so that they could memorize with their bodies the steps of the dance. Michaela does not need that. Her whole being is tuned to absorbing and transmitting the spirit within the physical actions of the dance. Her own spirit is free — free to put forth the emotions in the music, in the dance. People say to me, Make her a Spanish dancer; it is her gypsy inheritance. But that is not right. Michaela must be herself — as I was myself. She will be herself.

* * * * *

When the performance was over and the curtain calls taken, Julia continued to sit, carried out of the moment, until Laura touched her arm. They were seated in the middle of the row. Mrs. Rudolph and her party were already standing, ready to move along into the aisle. "Wake up, dear," said Laura, smiling at her absorption. "Our little girl does show promise, doesn't she? How clever of Lila to have seen it from the very beginning."

They hung back, allowing the crowd in the aisle to move slowly ahead out into the foyer. When they reached the outer doors, they stood back in a corner, out of the milling throng. The thought was in both their minds: they must see Michaela; tonight she would be gone with the dance troupe; her things were already out of the apartment. Lila they would see in the morning. At the moment she was undoubtedly backstage in the midst of an excited, chattering group of patrons, dancers, admirers who remembered her in her own days of glory, everyone stirred up by the brilliance of this evening. Florists' people were arriving with bouquets for the dancers. The air was heavy with the combined scent of perfume and hot-house blossoms. The babble of voices drowned out any conversation. They glimpsed Denise for a moment surrounded by ecstatic friends. But no Michaela.

Then the crowd began to thin out, flowing out into the street through the wide-open doors. The foyer began to darken. It was now almost empty and the main lights were out. Suddenly Laura saw that Michaela had emerged from the half-lit corridor. She wore warm trousers and a heavy sweater and carried the bag that held her dancing clothes. She came quickly to them and then stopped abruptly, looking from one to the other, her face glowing. Then all at once shy, she dropped her eyes and stood silent before them.

Julia said, putting her hand on Michaela's arm, "You were really wonderful, Michaela."

Michaela made a little sound, as if she wanted to say something but could not speak. As she hesitated, they heard someone unseen call from the corridor, "Michaela! Michaela! We're waiting for you!"

Michaela's body stiffened. As if galvanized by the sound of her name, she leaped forward and caught Laura in her arms, her kit bag swinging against Laura's legs. Laura gasped as the strong young arms seized her. Through the emotional agitation caused by the thrust of Michaela's vibrant body against her own, she heard Michaela say, "I love you! I will always love you!"

Laura, struck dumb, did not move. Michaela released her and seized Julia's hand in both her own and kissed it. She looked up, the full blaze of her black eyes meeting Julia's. "Madame Julie," she said and strove to say something more but failed. She hung there for a moment, her eyes fixed on Julia's. Then she turned away, running with swift grace out of their sight down the darkened corridor, as the voice once more called, "Michaela! Michaela! Are you coming?"

* * * * *

Julia closed the door of the apartment. The emotional drain of the evening had caught up with both of them and they did not speak. Julia stood quietly, still rapt by the vision of Michaela bounding about the stage as if it really belonged to her. Laura, moving restlessly about, saw the mail lying on the table by the door. She picked up an envelope with a French stamp and handed it to Julia.

Julia opened it and glanced without interest at

the letter. "It's from Mme. Guerin," she said. "She wants to know whether we are coming to stay with her again this summer."

Laura moved close to her and put her arms around her neck. She said softly, "Julie, Julie," and then, putting her head down on her shoulder murmured, "It seems such a long time ago, doesn't it?"

"Yes," said Julia, taking her in her arms with a contented sigh.

A few of the publications of
THE NAIAD PRESS, INC.
P.O. Box 10543 • Tallahassee, Florida 32302
Phone (904) 539-5965
Toll-Free Order Number: 1-800-533-1973
Mail orders welcome. Please include 15% postage.

MICHAELA by Sarah Aldridge. 256 pp. A "Sarah Aldridge" romance. ISBN 1-56280-055-8 $10.95

KEEPING SECRETS by Penny Mickelbury. 208 pp. A Gianna Maglione Mystery. First in a series. ISBN 1-56280-052-3 9.95

THE ROMANTIC NAIAD edited by Katherine V. Forrest & Barbara Grier. 336 pp. Love stories by Naiad Press women. ISBN 1-56280-054-X 14.95

UNDER MY SKIN by Jaye Maiman. 336 pp. A Robin Miller mystery. 3rd in a series. ISBN 1-56280-049-3. 10.95

STAY TOONED by Rhonda Dicksion. 144 pp. Cartoons — 1st collection since *Lesbian Survival Manual.* ISBN 1-56280-045-0 9.95

CAR POOL by Karin Kallmaker. 272pp. Lesbians on wheels and then some! ISBN 1-56280-048-5 9.95

NOT TELLING MOTHER: STORIES FROM A LIFE by Diane Salvatore. 176 pp. Her 3rd novel. ISBN 1-56280-044-2 9.95

GOBLIN MARKET by Lauren Wright Douglas. 240pp. A Caitlin Reece Mystery. 5th in a series. ISBN 1-56280-047-7 9.95

LONG GOODBYES by Nikki Baker. 256 pp. A Virginia Kelly mystery. 3rd in a series. ISBN 1-56280-042-6 9.95

FRIENDS AND LOVERS by Jackie Calhoun. 224 pp. Mid-western Lesbian lives and loves. ISBN 1-56280-041-8 9.95

THE CAT CAME BACK by Hilary Mullins. 208 pp. Highly praised Lesbian novel. ISBN 1-56280-040-X 9.95

BEHIND CLOSED DOORS by Robbi Sommers. 192 pp. Hot, erotic short stories. ISBN 1-56280-039-6 9.95

CLAIRE OF THE MOON by Nicole Conn. 192 pp. See the movie — read the book! ISBN 1-56280-038-8 10.95

SILENT HEART by Claire McNab. 192 pp. Exotic Lesbian romance. ISBN 1-56280-036-1 9.95

HAPPY ENDINGS by Kate Brandt. 272 pp. Intimate conversations with Lesbian authors. ISBN 1-56280-050-7 10.95

THE SPY IN QUESTION by Amanda Kyle Williams. 256 pp. 4th
Madison McGuire.   ISBN 1-56280-037-X   9.95

SAVING GRACE by Jennifer Fulton. 240 pp. Adventure and
romantic entanglement.   ISBN 1-56280-051-5   9.95

THE YEAR SEVEN by Molleen Zanger. 208 pp. Women surviving
in a new world.   ISBN 1-56280-034-5   9.95

CURIOUS WINE by Katherine V. Forrest. 176 pp. Tenth
Anniversary Edition. The most popular contemporary Lesbian
love story.   ISBN 1-56280-053-1   9.95

CHAUTAUQUA by Catherine Ennis. 192 pp. Exciting, romantic
adventure.   ISBN 1-56280-032-9   9.95

A PROPER BURIAL by Pat Welch. 192 pp. A Helen Black
mystery. 3rd in a series.   ISBN 1-56280-033-7   9.95

SILVERLAKE HEAT: A Novel of Suspense by Carol Schmidt.
240 pp. Rhonda is as hot as Laney's dreams.   ISBN 1-56280-031-0   9.95

LOVE, ZENA BETH by Diane Salvatore. 224 pp. The most talked
about lesbian novel of the nineties!   ISBN 1-56280-030-2   9.95

A DOORYARD FULL OF FLOWERS by Isabel Miller. 160 pp.
Stories incl. 2 sequels to *Patience and Sarah.*   ISBN 1-56280-029-9   9.95

MURDER BY TRADITION by Katherine V. Forrest. 288 pp. A
Kate Delafield Mystery. 4th in a series. ISBN 1-56280-002-7   9.95

THE EROTIC NAIAD edited by Katherine V. Forrest & Barbara Grier.
224 pp. Love stories by Naiad Press authors.   ISBN 1-56280-026-4   12.95

DEAD CERTAIN by Claire McNab. 224 pp. A Carol Ashton
mystery. 5th in a series.   ISBN 1-56280-027-2   9.95

CRAZY FOR LOVING by Jaye Maiman. 320 pp. A Robin Miller
mystery. 2nd in a series.   ISBN 1-56280-025-6   9.95

STONEHURST by Barbara Johnson. 176 pp. Passionate regency
romance.   ISBN 1-56280-024-8   9.95

INTRODUCING AMANDA VALENTINE by Rose Beecham.
256 pp. An Amanda Valentine Mystery. First in a series.
                                          ISBN 1-56280-021-3   9.95

UNCERTAIN COMPANIONS by Robbi Sommers. 204 pp.
Steamy, erotic novel.   ISBN 1-56280-017-5   9.95

A TIGER'S HEART by Lauren W. Douglas. 240 pp. A Caitlin
Reece mystery. 4th in a series.   ISBN 1-56280-018-3   9.95

These are just a few of the many Naiad Press titles — we are the oldest and
largest lesbian/feminist publishing company in the world. Please request a
complete catalog. We offer personal service; we encourage and welcome direct
mail orders from individuals who have limited access to bookstores carrying
our publications.